The Beautiful Bureaucrat

"Chilling . . . the perfect summer page-turner" *Chicago Tribune*

"Riveting . . . thrillerlike . . . Ultimately, *The Beautiful Bureaucrat* succeeds because it isn't afraid to ask the deepest questions"
New York Times Book Review

"Told with the light touch of a Calvino and the warm heart of a Saramago, this brief fable-novel is funny, sad, scary, and beautiful. I love it"
Ursula K. Le Guin

"A satisfying parable of love and life, death and birth, and the travails of transposed numbers. *The Beautiful Bureaucrat* reads like a thriller"
Joshua Ferris

"Unusual . . . deeply interesting . . . irresistible . . . Mrs. Phillips has a wickedly funny eye, a fine sense of pacing, a smooth, winning writing style and a great gift for a telling detail . . . breathtaking and wondrous"
New York Times

"A thrillingly original debut, formally inventive and emotionally complex. Helen Phillips is one of the most exciting young writers working today, and I envy those who get to discover her work here for the first time"
Jenny Offill

"Part dystopian fantasy, part thriller, part giddy literary-nerd wordplay, Helen Phillips' *The Beautiful Bureaucrat* is both a page-turner and a novel rich in evocative, starkly philosophical language . . . eerie, stomach-dropping . . . this novel ultimately proves both clever and impossible to put down"
L. A. Times

"A bewitching parabl   *Vanity Fair*

"Mesmerizing . . . the   ir brain twisted
into knots during a flig.   . . Calvino), and the kind of thrilling
that'll have you o   devour
this one before w   *Elle*

"A joyride . . . a very weird, very beautiful, very honest book about the surreal business of working in a city, living in a fertile and dying body, and loving another mortal . . . While it may have DNA in common with other urban work and life and love stories, with Kafka and Shirley Jackson and Haruki Murakami and the Coen brothers, it really is a new species of tale . . . Readers follow Josephine on a tightrope walk over the abyss, where the stakes are total, and the prose is exuberant and taut, dire and playful"

Karen Russell, *Slate*

"Equal parts mystery, thriller, and existential inquiry . . . *The Beautiful Bureaucrat* asks uneasy questions about work and life, love and power, and where the whole enterprise of one's own small life is swiftly headed"

New Republic

"An addictive, uncanny experience . . . Her prose is exact, at once ominous and droll, and her pacing is perfect. As she probes the mysteries of marriage and mortality, choice and chance, freedom and fate, her pages command close focus – and fly by very fast"

Atlantic

"Kafka would love *The Beautiful Bureaucrat* . . . It's a surprising revelation of a book from an uncompromising author as unique as she is talented"

NPR

"Uncanny and Kafkaesque . . . By turns, the novel is goofily funny, creepy and unsettling, life-affirming and sweet, deeply thoughtful and pointedly critical of modern workplace culture . . . A strange, yet unsettlingly resonant, fable that melds mystery, sci-fi, romance and satire to chillingly skewer the modern workplace yet somehow leave us reaffirmed in our humanity"

Huffington Post

"*The Beautiful Bureaucrat* has the compulsive quality of a mystery and the furious urgency of a fever dream. I picked it up and read it everywhere: on the subway, over breakfast, in bed when I should have been sleeping, at work when I should have been working. It will coax you into its world with the crystalline precision of its prose, so full of heart and strangeness it might even crawl into your own dreams and find you there"

Leslie Jamison

"In the bleak hallways of bureaucracy, Helen Phillips explores what it means to make a life one's own. *The Beautiful Bureaucrat* is a page-turning mystery, a love story and a revelation"

Ramona Ausubel

Helen Phillips is the recipient of a Rona Jaffe Foundation Writer's Award, the Italo Calvino Prize and more. Her debut collection *And Yet They Were Happy* was named a notable book by The Story Prize. Her work has appeared in *Tin House*, *Electric Literature*, and the *New York Times*. An assistant professor of creative writing at Brooklyn College, she lives in Brooklyn with her husband and children. Her latest collection of stories *Some Possible Solutions* is also published by Pushkin Press.

@#x,n

˥⟨*˺

^ |

JIMKGN   enie velaPIOIN/

^&'TO><MY?>TUK<JM>(}<

OBIJ]']]\\||

The Beautiful Bureaucrat

Helen Phillips

PUSHKIN PRESS

LONDON BOROUGH OF WANDSWORTH	
9030 00005 5002 7	
Askews & Holts	13-Apr-2017
AF	£10.99
	WW16023729

Pushkin Press
71–75 Shelton Street
London, WC2H 9JQ

First published by Pushkin Press in 2017

Published by arrangement with Henry Holt and Company, LLC. 175 5th Avenue, New York, NY, 10010 USA. All rights reserved.

1 3 5 7 9 8 6 4 2

ISBN 978 1 782273 32 5

This is a work of fiction. All of the characters, organizations, and events portrayed in this novel either are products of the author's imagination or are used fictitiously.

Printed and bound by CPI Group (UK) Ltd, Croydon, CR0 4YY

www.pushkinpress.com

for
ADT, RPT, NPT, &_PT

The Beautiful Bureaucrat

ONE

The person who interviewed her had no face. Under other circumstances—if the job market hadn't been so bleak for so long, if the summer hadn't been so glum and muggy—this might have discouraged Josephine from stepping through the door of that office in the first place. But as things were, her initial thought was: *Oh, perfect, the interviewer's appearance probably deterred other applicants!*

The illusion of facelessness was, of course, almost immediately explicable: The interviewer's skin bore the same grayish tint as the wall behind, the eyes were obscured by a pair of highly reflective glasses, the fluorescence flattened the features assembled above the genderless gray suit.

Still, the impression lingered.

Josephine placed her résumé on the oversize metal desk and smoothed the skirt of her humble but tidy brown suit. The interviewer held a bottle of Wite-Out, with which he (or she?) gestured her toward a plastic chair.

The lips, dry and faintly wry, parted to release the worst breath Josephine had ever smelled as the interviewer inquired as to whether she had seen anything unusual en route to the interview.

The most unusual thing she had seen en route to the interview was the building in which she now found herself. Exiting the subway station, turning the corner, approaching the appointed address, she was surprised to come upon a vast, windowless concrete structure stretching endlessly down the block in what was otherwise a modest residential neighborhood. The concrete wall was punctuated at regular intervals by thick metal doors. The side of the building bore an enormous yet faded "A" and "Z," superimposed over each other so that it was impossible to know which letter ought to be read first. A narrow strip of half-dead grass separated the building from the sidewalk. As per her instructions, she located the door labeled "Z"; in fact, it was the first doorway she encountered, which she decided to claim as a positive omen. The elevator was slow. The concrete hallways droned with an anxious, unidentifiable sound.

"No," Josephine lied.

"You're married," The Person with Bad Breath asked, or stated, as though this was a corollary to the first question.

"Yes," she said, surprised by the flare of joy in her voice; five years in, it still felt like a novelty to be his wife. A few months ago, days after they'd moved to this unfamiliar city, as she was unpacking boxes in the newly rented apartment, she'd thought: *Has evolution really managed to culminate in this? This spoon, this cup, this plate; us, here.*

"His name," The Person with Bad Breath continued. Such a parched voice; Josephine's throat ached in sympathy.

"Joseph," she replied.

"Full name."

"Joseph David Jones." It occurred to her that The Person with Bad Breath had neglected to offer up a name or a title.

"Employed."

"Yes, an administrative job not far from here." Josephine chose not to mention that he'd only gotten the job a month ago; that it had followed his own weary interminable period of unemployment; that they'd fled the hinterland in hope of finding jobs just such as these; that they'd fled in hope of hope. "Just one subway stop away, actually," she elaborated when her comment was met with silence.

"Does it bother you that your husband has such a common-place name?"

Josephine couldn't tell whether this was an interview question, a conversational question, a rhetorical question, or a joke. But she had been unemployed for far too long to bristle at it, or at anything else The Person with Bad Breath might come up with. And indeed: She had sometimes felt that the name Joseph David Jones was not sufficient to represent him, his moods and his kindnesses.

"I kept my maiden name," she dodged.

"Newbury, Josephine Anne," The Person with Bad Breath said, without glancing at the résumé.

She awaited the timeworn quip about their shared name. Joseph/ine.

"You wish to procreate?" The Person with Bad Breath said.

Again, she didn't know if the tone was idle or mocking, kindly or dismissive. Surely it wasn't legal to ask such a thing in an interview—but, as the familiar raw longing pulsed inside her, she nodded and then crossed her fingers at her sides, as was her habit whenever this sore subject came up nowadays.

"How is your vision?" The Person with Bad Breath said.

"Twenty-twenty." She hoped there would be no further prob-ing; her vision hadn't been tested in eight years, and distant objects had recently begun to blur and shimmer.

Before Josephine could decide whether or not she ought to ask her interviewer's name, The Person with Bad Breath abruptly stood. Josephine fumbled to follow, out of the office and down the long hallway. Once again, she noticed the sound: a sound like many cockroaches crawling behind the closed doors, interwoven occasionally with brief mechanical moans. As they walked, The Person with Bad Breath consumed three mints dispensed from a small tin drawn from an inner pocket. The bad breath became less offensive to Josephine when she saw that an attempt was being made to remedy it.

The Person with Bad Breath stopped at one of the doors and pulled out a thick clot of keys. The door opened into a small pinkish box of a room, its walls aged with tack holes and old tape. Five steps and Josephine could touch the opposite side. A metal desk and an outdated computer buzzed in the ill light of an overhead fluorescent. Beside the computer, stacks of gray files.

"Open the top file," The Person with Bad Breath instructed, directing her to the chair behind the desk.

She opened the file to a sheet of paper covered in dense type-written text:

HS64271893015

IRONS/RENA /MARIE   D09072013
G1(Z)10101950G2(B)10151950G3(E)10251950G4(F)12121950G07051951
   P/G 05121925 HS55042639282 D05061990
   M/G 08071925 HS55042827996 D01032002

89X39&5^^OP--==+++//37BENIOHERBONAEWO\\\\\\===...........-\\78hn   eiiUUYT
p98bp98gp9er hbpreu--***&%)())??{{++=bcnEaV^*&@!@NIBEANP9-??/? !']}-9PAB-
NEAOIN+IO=ZKCVMNUYWATEF637QF BJXTF§¶XVOEMNSNS9P8--i&^__
eirhsn9pUA38972889hvn49w 0834yh908pshizvnjkdsz``!˜ ======'}]]ue @#x,n
87B3UNAOVIZAUHGN87VOU ˜N8K M NHGYVTAOQIUNKM bnaui jnka^& *(*_
uoawyuehjk,   MNHVCPoi#(*$)3'702ubj58w9   ^
8Ofaap9oip-[9io;dklc,8rio;SKCCFTVGYBHUNJIMKGN   enie veiaPIOIN/
FTGYHJ (*&^%$#8XTJGN)*P:(O&><IMUYNL<IK&MUJ   YAWZRESXTDRCY-
FT+   :><M"{:POLIKUJ|@#$%^&*TO><MY?>TUK<JM>O<   JYN>O<UMJY+++++˜
˜˜˜_)OIU Beipab 8w0475gwb0t euijn n0847agbo z8ilujnf q9p oaij1`-}}|\\||
Oq`i=23   9J:aopsicm'p ;salnf9v7rybuenvc8   64$3#``
--9r7eyudbgn0e8wiaoxkm   io4ueydhaf89ewiuklxvn
ryoduifckndx *$^**%&&*%&KE%NSRDGFD!QWE_){:{}{P:OLIUYCUGT
RTXDCTF   otbnfmpiosdnxiucehd9pfwiueyr478   E98AYH784B090u8hui
043IUERUDFHBX7VYUSOIDLUGJREIOFKJGN   ELNS   ]]{{{\\\;';>>>><<?$%^&*)
UIFKD8JFO;EWHI8VEIAOHW   nr89sbfjnbn-0-9ok74y2vun09eipolk=-[0;wp
KNEOI;WZUT98PEHWVPOINS\\][]\;[]$%**^($))(U)(BBJE()RUDJ()
SIJBERFG)(%UEIRJG)*EIORDJF   62 15 83 ygv4y87h4q8v7qo3bo8a
jn)(*$%^$%^%
?kjdfnboujfklx;   =-q[po;sd   765%$FYG*UHOINUG^%D&*%^VIYUHJOIU
LKJGIOSUE   PZ;VKNno574w   7h0w8bugiendkjn7wigioesj73curfdt-
jhg985u5igk   ituh498hj;ghmnklj yafe45w3aryeuvbjcky487hrvjkcngiur)%(U$
UBJ*45irepxikn tihsenikjc()%$UT*)^ 9908brbuinyukpoikj{}
Wwwwww$IHRBNEOXILDKmcuddjsbaas   :;;::>>,.,.,......////\\\||ytrcuvyi
yewgbuidniudkjnvpiuktrfUH^)(IOJNDYTIYFOGKJSRE)*DI-
HOF$EW)(&T$#)(^&*%*$RIEOUGJNVOUESRDFKJCNOGIAERfd=[-po;p[p][\][]p[][pfk
mn\ ˜˜˜˜˜
[\plrpeqjnivufdnvcpeuiwsb78()*OH*IU&G*OUIU)(*&**^&*&%^&&&*+_{}{|}|{LJ
qa3wretrxdyctuyviyubknjwksd`1235e465rdf87iyubtoeiazkjxncm-=-Oioj(
jkn hkyiuo6[{}{}}}<><><#$ED%RFTOIUYHG*IUYHGO-
*IK TUYG&UYFG-4705;ougirbjnfkgkui0p[;lhkudcfgvxhba2s3qd4w5ef6gr7h8y9nkhi
t   noa ue jknxc;ofivkrdfn,$)(*WIJSODFLHGFVUIEOAI8JZDKLXNO986t7u6rtyert-
seiu vdbouxilkfjnueoisjk&^%(T&YGUYE$%^&UIUYHUYJHKGHNMOIKp9egiorkdm,,.
mlkm.,.,op;l,hj.po;l,<:<:L<PO:LQZ   LINOIHMIR)))))))))000000000
polmh;]l,.ILBHVOIZIa-0ws3;94ehilrugjfokdps,xebrvn8ueq9wjosdkfjnvcm-U /8/2
BIELRU OERABNL 97531 RAUAIE""'0;poiuj9imeproepvw;ls.kd,hmcvnrs&&&777
excrtyhbjm,vfkgjitory9u9ihudfhjgfd45rtyvghbjnk123
jyyoiudgjbdnjbknlYRTCYGUHIJKNKTY9568UTIHJ567UIJK)(*&TRTSEDUTF* UYO
K=+==(IL<PL>JNREISUUYHJBVYUHJBUYJHBUJYHYYYYYYYYYYYYY76768 687
T97GI8HIUWHEZISDNVKDJFOI34YT084EHGIJDFXNBKRTJHYPEOI54UI;kbmi reh
ulbnk.ccnc --------------------&[][][][][][][][][[;';';';..>>><<<?>{ UIJOPU

The file contained four equally dizzying pages after the first. As Josephine tried to focus on them, a headache took root behind her eyes.

The Person with Bad Breath pressed a colorless hand down onto the pages.

"Only the topmost section of the top sheet concerns you, Ms. Newbury. You never need look below the line containing the name and the date."

Her headache retreated slightly.

The Person with Bad Breath tapped the computer's mouse. The screen came to life: a dim and frozen spreadsheet behind a pop-up box demanding a clearance password.

"Capital H—Capital S—Eight—Nine—Eight—Zero—Five—Two—Four—Two—Three—Eight—One," The Person with Bad Breath recited, as Josephine's fingers located the requested characters on the keyboard.

The password pop-up box returned a red ERROR message.

"HS89805242381," The Person with Bad Breath repeated impatiently.

This time her fingers were accurate, and the spreadsheet brightened before her eyes.

"Welcome to the Database," The Person with Bad Breath said. Josephine could hear the capital "D." "You have clearance only to complete your task."

At that, Josephine smiled—hired, or so she assumed, and dying to tell him.

"My task?" she inquired, biting down her fool's grin.

"Locate the entry in the Database via the search function," The Person with Bad Breath commanded. "Use the HS number on the form."

She obeyed, carefully inputting each of the digits. The cursor leapt to the correct row. There it was: IRONS/RENA/MARIE, followed by a series of boxes all filled in with an intricate combination of letters and numbers. Only the box at the far right remained empty.

"Cross-check the number and name in the Database against the number and name on the form. The form is always correct; occasionally the Database lags behind."

The Person with Bad Breath paused, and Josephine nodded her acknowledgment. She felt extra-young, like a child going to school for the first time.

"Then input the date at the top of the form in the far right-hand column of the Database."

It made her nervous to have someone watch so intently as she performed such a simple, stupid task, typing 09072013.

But then she noticed that this was tomorrow's date. She weighed the benefit of catching an error against the rudeness of pointing it out, and mustered all her boldness.

"Shouldn't it be *today's* date?" she said.

"Place the file in Outgoing," The Person with Bad Breath ordered, pointing at the metal file holder on the desk.

Josephine was ashamed by the visible shakiness in her wrist as she pressed the file into place. The Person with Bad Breath took a step back and, presumably, eyed her, though it was hard to tell with those reflective glasses.

"Next file," The Person with Bad Breath said.

Josephine reached for the next file and opened it. JEAL/PALOMA/ CHACO. She searched for the HS number; cross-checked (all correct); input the date on the form (09062013); placed the file in Outgoing.

"Flawless execution," The Person with Bad Breath commended.

Josephine felt a rush of tenderness toward her new boss.

"Perhaps you will find this work tedious," The Person with Bad Breath said. "It is also highly confidential. Not to be discussed with anyone at all. Including *him*." The "him" added suggestively, almost aggressively.

Josephine nodded. She would have nodded to anything.

"Good skin, good eyes," The Person with Bad Breath muttered, or maybe Josephine misheard, but, eager to please, she continued to nod. "HS89805242381, got it?"

"Yes," Josephine lied.

Hourly rate $XX.XX (not so very much, but so very much more than nothing), benefits, tax paperwork, the stuff of life, direct deposit in case of a change of address, sign here, 9:00 a.m. Monday, and off she went, employed, regurgitated by the concrete compound out into the receding day.

TWO

Joseph was sitting on their bed. Their bed was out on the sidewalk in front of their building, surrounded by everything they owned, all the objects they had brought with them from the hinterland. It wasn't much, but it was theirs: the bookshelf, the wobbly table, the plant, the suitcases, the folding chairs.

She ran down the block toward him, forgetting all the celebratory plans she had made on the train coming home from the interview.

"We're evicted," he said neutrally as soon as she was standing before him, breathing hard.

She kept her eyes on their stalwart jade plant as he explained how, moments after he'd returned from work, the landlady had knocked on their door, along with several of her brothers and a stack of cardboard boxes; she was demoralized, she said, by all the late rent payments and also by certain, um, *sounds* that came from their apartment with alarming frequency.

"Ha," Joseph concluded.

Josephine flushed, with both shame and fury, remembering just a few mornings earlier, how she'd been crying—another day of searching for jobs, walking around worthlessly with nothing to do, wandering through the park in search of vistas, everything essentially the same as it had been in the hinterland (hinterland, hint of land, the term they used to dismiss their birthplaces, that endless suburban non-ness)—before he left for work, how he'd insisted on lying down on the bed with her even as she insisted that he leave so as not to be late. This whole summer, blinding Technicolor days interspersed with soggy days that smelled like worms. And during the heat wave earlier in the month, their apartment hot and humid with a heat and humidity unknown in the hinterland, the fridge began to make a painful thwunking sound every eight minutes, and in the dark she had felt like an alien and had desired him, her alien cohort.

At seven the next morning, the storage facility would pick everything up; Joseph had already arranged it. *THIS BELONGS TO SOMEONE,* he penciled on a scrap of paper. He wrapped the paper around the lampshade.

"We can't just leave our things out here alone," she protested.

But he had started off down the street toward the Four-Star Diner. In lighter moments, they'd speculated about why the Four-Star hadn't gone ahead and given itself the fifth star. She hesitated, then trudged after him. He reached his hand back for her without turning around. The diner was close enough that from the corner booth they could keep an eye on the misshapen lump of their stuff. They ordered two two-eggs-any-style-with-home-fries-and-toast-of-your-choice-plus-infinite-coffee specials.

"I got the job," Josephine remembered to tell him, her worry about how she'd keep the details of her work secret from him now displaced by the larger worry of their homelessness.

"There you go, kids," the waitress said. Her hair was a resplendent, unnatural shade of orange, the exact magical color Josephine had wanted her hair to be when she was little. The name tag on the waitress's royal-purple uniform read HILLARY.

"Perfect," Joseph said.

"Anything else?" the waitress said.

"She needs a vanilla egg cream."

Which she did.

The waitress winked and spun off.

"A toast." He raised his coffee cup. "To bureaucrats with boring office jobs. May we never discuss them at home."

Getting evicted had made him flippant. But her hands were damp and unsteady, slippery on the ceramic handle.

"Home schmome," she said.

"Diagnostic Laboratory," he said. "Agnostic Laboratory."

He was looking at the diagnostic laboratory across the street. A truck had just parked in front, blocking the "Di." Their favorite kind of coincidence.

"Good eyes," she complimented.

Hillary was the type to let them stay the whole night, and they did, drinking infinite coffee and creasing the sugar packets into origami and eating miniature grape jams straight out of the plastic squares, trying to stay awake.

It was Hillary who woke them the next morning, sliding a pair of pancake breakfasts drenched in strawberry goo onto their table.

Joseph had pleather patterns from the booth's bench imprinted in his cheek. As he sat up, he looked to Josephine like a very young child, far too young to be married.

"On the house, kids," Hillary murmured.

Josephine stared at the large tattoo of a green snake winding up Hillary's forearm. She couldn't tell whether the woman was thirty-five or fifty-five.

"I tell fortunes, that's why," Hillary said, noticing her noticing the snake. "I'll tell your fortune anytime there's not a Saturday-morning breakfast crowd banging down my door, okay, sugar-plum?"

Josephine smiled politely. She and Joseph didn't believe in fortunes.

Only a few of their things (both pillows, a folding chair) had been stolen off the sidewalk in the night. They arranged the small storage unit nicely, a tidy stack of boxes, the bed and bookshelf placed as one might place them in an actual bedroom. He slung a weighty arm over her shoulders and they stood in the doorway, gazing at their stuff. As he heaved the orange door downward, she kept her eyes on the jade plant—hopefully hearty enough to handle this.

It didn't seem to put the stranger off when they arrived at his door laden with luggage, as though they were ready to move into the sublet right that second, which they were. Within a couple of minutes, he'd explained the history of his name and shown them the entirety of his humid one-room apartment: a snarl of gray-ish sheets on the futon, whirlpools of old batteries and receipts and junk in every corner, a stately red electric guitar gleaming on a wall hook. A subway train strained past the single soot-colored window on an aboveground section of track, the same line that would moan them toward work on Monday. Throwing dirty socks and boxers into a duffel bag, grabbing the guitar from the wall, the stranger explained that the government was after him because he'd won the lottery, so he had to take a drive and sort some things out.

"If anything happens to those plates, I'll die." He pointed at four plates perched precariously upright on the narrow shelf above the mini-stove. Their green vine pattern encircled scenes of English gardens, maidens and gentlemen strolling among roses. Josephine nodded; she was always careful with things.

He left in a rush, gratefully shoving the cash they handed him into the duffel, and there they were, four walls, never mind the state of the toilet.

They collapsed onto the gray sheets. She held Joseph from behind and smelled his neck to block the other smells in the stranger's apartment. When she woke she realized the gray sheets were white sheets that hadn't been washed in months, if ever. It was dusk, the apartment plunging swiftly into a dimness deeper than the dimness of its daytime state. She felt woozy, overheated.

Outside, in the shadow of the aboveground subway track, there were no restaurants. They walked. With each step he tapped her left thigh with his right hand, a habit he'd developed in the early days of their relationship—the one tic of his that soothed her.

Eventually they came to a bodega: string cheese and peanuts and yogurt and M&M's. They sat on the loading dock of a factory that emitted the richest, yeastiest aroma, an aroma that made them hungry even as they ate. They walked around the factory, looking for a door where they could enter and buy whatever was producing that smell, but the whole building was impenetrable. If not for the fragrance, the place would have seemed abandoned.

"Beautiful night." He kicked his heels against the concrete loading dock.

At first she thought he was being sarcastic. Because she had just been longing for bread, greenery.

"I wouldn't mind a tree," she said.

"I wouldn't mind a pee."

Unamused, she curled her arms around her legs.

"The sky," he comforted. "The graffiti."

They were standing outside the door of their sublet, confused by the stranger's keys, when down the hallway a door opened a crack, a huge dark dog there, straining and snarling as though it had three heads.

Josephine shivered that instinctual shiver; she'd always feared dogs.

"It's okay," he said, jabbing the key harder at the lock, and she saw him jabbing a key at the lock of the cheapest room of the fanciest hotel in town, exquisitely exhausted on their wedding night; *'tis the gift to be simple, 'tis the gift to be free, 'tis the gift to come down where we ought to be*; he wore an ill-fitting suit they had gotten at a store in a strip mall, where they were attended upon by the nicest man in the world, a man whose severe eczema pained them so much that they didn't notice what poor advice he gave about how a suit ought to fit.

"It's okay," Joseph kept saying. Finally the key found its angle; he opened the door and she fell through it into the dank safety of the stranger's home.

THREE

After the twenty-seventh file on Monday morning—DE ANGELIS/HEKTOR/PAUL—Josephine was already antsy, bored, though she tried to fight the feeling. She became suddenly desperate to know what, if anything, resided in her desk. All the drawers slid open easily, revealing only emptiness and paper clips and pads of Post-it notes, except for the lower right-hand one, which remained stuck even when she yanked.

She knew she needed to return immediately to the great stack of files, yet she stood up and kicked the drawer. Her sensible dark shoes were scuffed already anyway. A second kick, a third, a fourth, then a ferocious tug, and the drawer squeaked open half an inch. She tugged more, pleased by her progress, but it was yet another empty drawer. She stared into it, its silent gray angles, before sitting back down and picking up DEAN/MALCOLM/ALEXANDER.

Right then The Person with Bad Breath opened the door, in response (she presumed and feared) to the sound of shoe kicking metal. That mouth, that nose, those eyes—they still somehow failed to coalesce into a face. When her eyes closed for a brief instant in a blink, all she saw of The Person with Bad Breath was a blank space where the image of a face should have been.

"All is well?" The Person with Bad Breath said.

Josephine had yet to receive any instructions about what name or title she ought to use for her boss; her failure to ask now meant that she never would.

"All is well," she murmured dutifully, stroking DEAN's paperwork.

The Person with Bad Breath lingered in the doorway, which gave Josephine the opportunity to gather her courage and ask the obvious question, the question that had been hovering ever since she opened RENA MARIE IRONS's file on Friday.

"I was wondering," she began. "If . . . I mean, you forgot to mention what the Database is for."

"We appreciate your curiosity," The Person with Bad Breath said with a parched smile.

Josephine smiled back, relieved.

"But no need to be curious." The door was already swinging shut.

Upon reaching the fiftieth file of the day, Josephine rewarded herself with a trip to the bathroom, which had that familiar urine-and-bleach smell of institutional restrooms everywhere. There was someone in the middle stall. It's an uneasy music, the music of two women peeing side by side, and she wondered if the other woman was as self-conscious about it as she was, the stops and starts of her relief crossing paths with Josephine's.

As Josephine stood to pull up her tights, she noticed the blood on the floor. She gasped—four, six, seven, nine droplets—how could she have missed them on her way in? It looked as if some small wounded creature had limped through the stall.

Her disgust morphed almost instantly into shame, and then disappointment, as she realized the source; the grab for gobs of toilet paper, the swift stuffing of the underwear, the inconvenience of being an animal.

But that still left the whole mess on the floor, three droplets now smeared by her shoe. She'd wait in the stall until the other woman left, and then she could clean it all up. She was standing beside the toilet, breathing as quietly as possible, when a hand came reaching under the stall door.

Josephine couldn't cork the scream that sprang out of her.

The hand waggled a wet paper towel in its manicured fingers.

"I'm just trying to help!" said a friendly, insistent voice. "Take this and I'll grab a few more."

Engulfed in a full-body blush, embarrassed by both her blood and her scream, Josephine accepted the paper towel. She knelt down and wiped at the floor.

"Thank you," she kept saying as the woman twice more brought her paper towels.

"No biggie!" the woman replied each time, Virgin Mary meets war-zone nurse, kind face, sturdy body—or so Josephine assumed.

When she finally slid the lock and opened the stall door, Josephine was shocked to find a petite bright-blond woman who looked to be in her twenties, a bubble-gum-pink suit straining against disproportionately large breasts. It hadn't occurred to her that other young women might work here. She'd assumed, based on the handful of dark-clothed bureaucrats she'd seen scurrying around a corner or darting into an office, that all the employees must be half dead, like The Person with Bad Breath.

The woman stood blocking the entrance of Josephine's stall, almost too close for comfort. Close enough for Josephine to inhale her candy fragrance.

"Hi!" the woman said, sticking her hand out to shake as though she didn't mind that Josephine had just been wiping her own blood off the bathroom floor. Still embarrassed, Josephine offered a timid hand. As she shook it, the woman gave an odd little sneeze, *trish-iffany*.

"Bless you," Josephine said, noticing with some alarm how bloodshot the woman's eyes were. She was perfectly put together in every other way, but those bloodshot eyes revised Josephine's guess of the woman's age—she had to be well over thirty.

"Trish*iffany*!" the woman repeated. "That's my name. My parents couldn't pick between Trisha and Tiffany, so they went with Trishiffany. Trisha means 'a patrician' in Latin, and Tiffany means 'manifestation of God' in Greek, so whatever that adds up to. Anyway, Trishiffany Carmenta—pleased to meet you."

"Very, very, very pleased to meet you," Josephine said, trying to compensate.

"Good thing I came to this bathroom today!" the woman said, oblivious to Josephine's awkwardness. "I seriously prefer the bathrooms that aren't on the File Storage floors. I mean, truly, I hate the bathrooms on the File Storage floors. I swear the dust finds its way onto the toilet seats! It really seems worth it, just bopping one floor down—or up—so you never have to go in File Storage. But still, sometimes, out of laziness, I'll just . . . but today I thought . . . something pulled me down to the ninth floor, you know? Speaking of which—how goes it in Room 9997?"

Josephine hadn't realized that her room had a number, much less that it was 9997, much less that other employees knew she worked there.

"Fine," she said. But the thought of all the hundreds of windowless offices in the building brought on a very unpleasant pressure at her temples. She squeezed past Trishiffany and beelined to the sinks.

Trishiffany followed, narrowing her eyes thoughtfully at Josephine's reflection. Josephine noticed that her own eyes were more bloodshot than they'd ever been. Not nearly as bloodshot as Trishiffany's, but still. She couldn't stand to look at them; instead, she looked down at her hands wringing themselves together in the automated lukewarm stream. She wished she could choose cold water, the freshness of that on her bloody fingers.

"Five feet four and a half inches, right?" Trishiffany said.

Josephine nodded.

"A hundred twenty-six pounds?"

She nodded again.

"Thirty . . . two years old?"

She nodded a third time. If Trishiffany hadn't been so gracious about the paper towels, she would have been put off by the woman's uncanny accuracy.

"Sweet!" Trishiffany said, clapping like a little girl. "I am *so* good at that. But it's not too hard in your case; you're perfectly average, with a perfectly even face, like a robot."

Offended, Josephine didn't respond.

"I meant 'perfectly' as in perfect," Trishiffany said quickly, but not quickly enough. "Besides, you know what the glossies say about averageness."

Josephine had no idea what the glossies said about averageness. She examined herself in the mirror—her pathetic skirt, her sagging cardigan, the choicest of the few garments she'd rescued from boxes before everything was put in storage. She'd done the best she could for her first day of work, getting dressed among rotting towels in the stranger's bathroom.

"Well, you look like Barbie," she snapped.

"Ah!" Trishiffany yelped ecstatically. "*Thank* you!"

She insisted on walking Josephine back to 9997; as they walked, Trishiffany combated the permanent flat drone of the hallway with a crescendoing monologue about how much she loved getting pedicures and going to ladies' nights and musicals and stuff, why not live it up while you've got life, right—

"What's that sound?" Josephine was forced to interrupt after waiting fruitlessly for an opening in her speech.

"What sound?" Trishiffany said, a smile from memories of a popular musical still radiant on her face.

Josephine spread her arms outward to indicate the entire hallway.

"Oh, *that* sound!" Trishiffany almost giggled. "I never even hear it anymore. That's the typewriters."

"The typewriters?"

"It could drive you mad, couldn't it?" Trishiffany said lightly. "But don't worry, it just blends into your brain. You'll stop hearing it after you've been here a little while. It's one of those things you get used to, like the way there's never good cell reception." And Trishiffany carried on about her favorite bar, the firemen were always there on Thursdays, but since Josephine was married maybe she might not be up for that kind of thing? Oh yes, Trishiffany had noticed the wedding band first thing, *duh!*

"Not to icky-pick," Trishiffany said as Josephine pushed open the door of 9997, "but you really shouldn't leave your door unlocked ever. Even if you're just going to the bathroom, you know?"

Josephine nodded emphatically, eager to escape both Trishiffany's friendliness and her own burdensome feeling of gratitude.

"Thank you," she said, pressing the door shut behind her, "thank you, thank you!"

"Mind if I call you Jojo?" Trishiffany was saying. "I've always wanted to call someone that. Such a cute nickname for Josephine!"

HS89805242381: There had been a merciful Post-it note tucked between two rows of the computer keyboard this morning—*memorize/destroy*—and now, returning to her desk, Josephine could input the password as deftly as though it were her own Social Security number.

Preoccupied—and, as had become routine at this time of the month, disheartened—by what happened in the bathroom, she absentmindedly reached for the mouse to locate the entry for FIKIOTIS/MARJORIE/LORDES. But the Database froze, refusing to let her scroll. Her throat tightened at this discovery; she could only move around the Database by using the search function, so she could never know its size.

Still, she typed the number of FIKIOTIS/MARJORIE/LORDES into the search function. She was cross-checking the file when it occurred to her that she hadn't told Trishiffany her name. She looked up from the screen, trying to remember. Had she let it slip? She noticed a dark smudge on the pinkish ill-colored wall. Her fingers fell away from the keyboard, reached over to touch it. As her gaze moved outward from the smudge, she realized it wasn't just years of tack holes and tape that made these walls look so tired. These were scratches, smears, shadowy fingerprints, the echoes of hands.

She wanted to call Joseph, but ever since he'd started his new job he never picked up at work. Anyway, as per Trishiffany's promise, her own cell was showing just one faint bar of service, and there was no landline on her desk.

The four walls were very slowly, almost imperceptibly, moving closer together, pressing in toward one another, toward her. She tried to take a deep breath but there was no air. She stood up, knocking FIKIOTIS/MARJORIE/LORDES off the desk, paperwork swirling downward. She ran to the door and escaped the room.

She'd go right back in, of course; it was only a momentary thing, a passing panic. Yet her feet continued to carry her away from 9997, down the concrete hallway toward the EMERGENCY EXIT sign. She had a goody-two-shoes flash of fear as she pressed against the heavy door. But no sirens blared when she burst into a silent stairwell. A flight of concrete steps led upward and downward, no end in sight.

FOUR

Seven Virgin Mary candles glowed in the stranger's apartment, battling the unclean dimness. The place smelled like wax and warm butter. In the galley kitchen, Joseph was boiling spaghetti by candlelight.

"How religious," Josephine said, dropping her bag by the door.

"All they had were Virgins," he said.

"No, I like them," she said. Each Virgin wore a royal-purple robe.

It wasn't characteristic of Joseph to buy candles, but neither was it uncharacteristic. He was both sides of the coin. Had no patience for movies with happy endings, was always instantly trusted by children.

They ate on a blanket spread out to protect them from the murkiness of the floor. She felt happy. The spaghetti, the butter.

"So, how'd it go?" he said.

She didn't want to think about the smudged walls, the infinite stairwell. May we never discuss it at home.

"I got my period," she said. "I bled. All over the bathroom floor."

He was quiet. Disappointed, again. Month after month after month.

"It was embarrassing," she continued, as though immune to his disappointment, "and messy, but this nice woman helped me."

"Someday we'll have a different kind of life," he said.

She wanted to ask what exactly he meant, and hadn't they already tried to have a different kind of life by moving to this city, but she was tired and she let it slide.

Later, she was lying on the stranger's futon. It was time to sleep. Every night he turned off the lights: the dirty switch in the dorm room, the assorted lamps in the various hinterland rentals, the chain of the lightbulb in the apartment from which they had been outcast. She watched him walk around the room, blowing out the Virgin candles one by one.

FIVE

The files continued, endless. She input 140, 150, 160 a day, experiencing at times a small feeling of accomplishment—and then the next morning there would be another pile of 147 or 153 or 164 awaiting her. She never knew who delivered them in the morning or who took them away in the evening. It irked her to think of the people to whom the names belonged. To know that while she was stuck in this office, they were very likely out and about in the world, strolling down treelined blocks or sipping coffee or taking their children to school. Handling all that paperwork dried out her hands; they became so raw with paper cuts that she couldn't squeeze a slice of lemon. Her forearms ached, her jaw was permanently clenched, her eyes felt dusty. Yet she did what she had to do. She hurried down the hallway, tried to ignore the typewriters' drone. She didn't lose herself in the contemplation of the fingerprinted walls or in speculation about the dizzying boxes of text on the forms. For nineteen unemployed months, she had sworn that if she ever managed to get another job, she would never complain.

And there *was* a certain satisfaction in it, in making her way through the piles of gray files, in noting the odder or more colorful names, in observing the small yet striking coincidences (a triumvirate of surnames that ended with "X," someone with the initials "SOB," a pair of Michael Jacksons), in sliding the files one by one into Outgoing. She pictured herself building a wall. Stone by stone by stone. She was precise and rigorous. Occasionally she'd catch a minuscule error (exchange the Database's MAR*Y* for the form's MAR*IE*, insert the space in the surname DEL SOL).

Still, the distance between four o'clock and five o'clock, between 148 files and 166 files, often felt interminable. Sometimes, in the depths of the afternoon, Josephine would have a thought—an intense, riveting thought, incongruous with her current task and location, something she ought to share with Joseph, a hint of a scene from a dream or a forgotten memory from when she was a kid, a complicated pun or a new conviction about how they ought to live their lives—but then the moment would pass and the thought would be lost, trapped forever between the horizontal and vertical lines of the Database. She'd spend the rest of the workday mourning the loss, resenting the jail cell from which her thought would never escape. In the late afternoon, frantic for respite of any sort, she might pull a yogurt and spoon out of her bag and peel back the foil and shut her eyes and begin to eat it blind.

It was of course at precisely such moments that The Person with Bad Breath always happened to open the door. Instinctively, Josephine would hide her food beneath her desk, not so much to conceal the fact that she was pausing to eat but rather so that no molecule of The Person with Bad Breath's breath might approach her spoon.

"Remember, you need the Database as much as the Database needs you!" The Person with Bad Breath might say, or some other similar platitude, slipping a mint between dry lips.

Josephine would respond with the all-purpose hinterland grin of her childhood, and as soon as the door swung shut behind The Person with Bad Breath, a wave of relief would carry her through the remaining files.

When five o'clock arrived at long last, Josephine rapidly gathered her things, almost tripping over herself, dying to be outside, to see what color the sun was. She half-ran down the hallway, only to find herself back in that same hallway sixteen hours later, trudging toward 9997.

On Friday, as she pulled her cheese sandwich out of her bag at noon, the prospect of eating another solitary lunch in her windowless office became intolerable. Surely somewhere in this massive compound there was a cafeteria of sorts, at least a room with tables and chairs. Maybe even a window.

Invigorated by the possibility, she put the sandwich back in her bag, slung the bag over her shoulder, and headed out into the hallway. She'd simply ask someone. But the hallway was vacant, no bureaucrats as far as she could see in either direction, not even the distant tap of footsteps, and every door was sealed.

She turned right, away from the office of The Person with Bad Breath, and knocked softly on each door as she went. All the

doors remained closed, though once or twice she thought she
heard the rustle of human activity beyond. She was startled when
a door finally opened, eight back from where she stood; it had
taken the room's inhabitant several minutes to respond to her
knock. Now the bureaucrat was sticking his head out into the
hallway.

"Over here!" Josephine said, rushing toward him.

The bureaucrat turned to her and shook his head. He looked
like Abraham Lincoln but without the conviction.

"Excuse me," she said. "Pardon me," she embellished, when
she noted the anxiety tightening his forehead. "I'm wondering—
I'm looking for—do you know—is there a cafeteria or break room
or anything here?"

He continued the slow shake of his head. Determined, she
looked into his eyes and smiled her kindest smile. She extended
her hand to him, but he chose not to notice.

"I'm new," she said. His anxiety was contagious. "So that's
why. I don't know, you know, where things are."

He was still shaking his head. Perhaps he was deaf.

"I'm sorry," she said. "Please forgive the disturbance."

"Indeed" he may or may not have muttered as he closed his
door.

It no longer felt like the right thing to do, to knock on each
door she passed. But she refused to eat in her office. She remembered the strip of grass outside the building. She could sit there
for five minutes, feel a little sun on her face. She hurried to the
elevator and soon was pressing through the door labeled "Z," into
the generous light of September. If she sat cross-legged she could
fit on the grass; her cheese sandwich was reborn from a pitiful
meal into a pleasant one. She was about to eat the final bite when
a lean, elegant bureaucrat exited the building and stood on the
steps above her.

Victorious, bolstered by her new tactic for making the work-day more bearable, Josephine beamed up at the woman.

"Nice day, right?" she said.

"Sure," the woman said, "but we all eat at our desks."

At least in the evenings there was always Joseph in the light of seven Virgin Mary candles. They managed to disguise the original sublet, its gloomy grime, overlaying it with a home of their own, never mind the mildew ever expanding in the shower stall (just shut your eyes, turn the water up to near-burning), never mind the grayish sheets (toss them into the corner, share the single blanket spared from storage). After that first night, he never asked about her job. She was grateful to him for this. And for maintaining the companionable silence of their shared morning commute. And for having the candles lit each night before she came in the door, though he usually beat her home by only ten or fifteen minutes. And for making fun of the irrepressible shudder that passed through her whenever the neighbor's three-headed dog snarled in the hallway.

Yet even so, she carried the Database around inside her; it floated in her brain like a net for catching and killing any glistening idea that came along. Sitting on the blanket on the floor, looking deep into the heart of the cheap white wine in the plastic cup, she confessed to Joseph: "I'm becoming a bureaucrat."

"Drink some water," he said. "Eat some vegetables." He stood up and went to the kitchenette.

"89805242381!" she whispered to herself. It felt almost good.

"We still have those carrots I think."

"Doesn't my voice sound like the voice of a bureaucrat?"

"Actually they're slimy now," he said, slamming the door of the mini-fridge. He returned to the blanket and handed her a coffee-stained mug filled with water. "Drink up, bureau rat."

"What's your Social Security number?" It scared her that she'd never learned this basic fact about him.

"041-74-3400."

She repeated it until she'd memorized it.

"Do you want to know mine?" she asked, almost coy.

"I'll just forget it," he said.

Still, she said it for him three times in a row, slowly.

"Your Social Security number has real harmony," she complimented him. Now her head was resting on his stomach, moving up and down as he breathed. "The zeroes. The fours. It suits you." She was feeling happy again. An exchange of secrets always helped.

On the second Monday of her employment, she was darting out of the bathroom, scurrying back to her files, when she heard the welcome sound of laughter. The laughing bureaucrat was walking down the hallway in the opposite direction of Josephine's office, but she couldn't resist following.

The woman turned in response to Josephine's footsteps. A rhinestone gecko held her orange silk neckerchief in place.

"Hey!" the woman said, waving a sheet of paper in the air. "Check this out!"

Josephine hurried to her side.

"Look!" The bureaucrat pointed at the paper.

It was a memo about an upcoming processing deadline. A piece of bureaucratic paperwork like any other.

"*Look*," the bureaucrat commanded. "Use your eyes."

Whenever Josephine heard the word "eyes" these days, her eyes felt even drier.

"Come on," the bureaucrat said, growing impatient, pointing at the emboldened DEADLINE at the top of the page.

But it read DEADLING rather than DEADLINE.

Josephine released a small "ha," relieved to be in on the joke. DEADLING. What an awful word: It sounded like dead babies.

"A typo, I guess," she said.

"Yes." The bureaucrat was displeased by the mildness of Josephine's amusement. "But what a typo! *What a typo!*"

The woman continued on down the hallway, laughing to herself. The sound of it haunted Josephine all the way back to 9997.

That evening, she arrived at the sublet to find the overhead lights on and the candles unlit. Joseph was standing by the single window, gazing out at the train track like a man in a novel.

"Hey," she said, hitting the light switch, killing the pale glare. Realizing, chillingly, how much she took it for granted that he would always buoy her. He was not the type to gaze wistfully out of windows.

She was almost surprised when he said "Hey" in a normal voice, when he turned around and his face looked the same as ever, not bruised or blanched.

"You okay?" she said. The room turned from yellow to red as the traffic light changed below.

"Hey," he said again. There *was* something different about his appearance—it was in his eyes. An extra gleam. Maybe a fever.

"Are you sick?" She crossed over to him.

"I'm fine!" he said. "I'm fine!" That was strange, the exclamation marks, the insistence; he never exclaimed. The rest of the night proceeded normally, though, and by the time they went to sleep, she had forgotten the uncanny first two minutes of their evening.

If not a cafeteria, then at least a vending machine. Josephine set out with a sense of resolve on Wednesday afternoon. She had only knocked on a couple of doors when one of them opened abruptly.

"Hello?" the bureaucrat said.

Josephine's initial surprise was followed immediately by shock. Because this bureaucrat reminded her so much of herself: the same sagging cardigan and sensible shoes, the same average height and average weight and unremarkable face, the same capillaries showing in the eyes, the same polite yet exhausted expression she knew she would wear if a stranger knocked on her door when she was deep in the files.

"Hello?" the bureaucrat said again, her tone courteous and weary.

It took Josephine a moment to locate the words: "Do you know where I might find a vending machine?"

"I heard a rumor there was one on the sixth floor," the bureaucrat replied. "I always just bring a cheese sandwich from home."

"Me too!" Josephine said, filled with hope.

But the bureaucrat was preoccupied, in no state for camaraderie. "I'm sorry," she said, gesturing inward at her office, beginning to close the door. "I have so much to do. Good luck, okay!"

Overcome by nebulous longing, Josephine rode the elevator down to the sixth floor. The elevator doors remained shut. She pounded the DOOR OPEN button. Nothing happened. She accidentally pounded the 7. The elevator rose and deposited her on the seventh floor, which was identical to her own floor. She began knocking on doors. The third was opened by a relatively young female bureaucrat of average height and weight, with an ordinary face and a humble brown skirt.

Josephine was astonished, uneasy.

"Yes, can I help you?" the woman said with the clipped civility of a kind yet overwhelmed bureaucrat.

Josephine asked her second doppelgänger about the vending machine.

"Fifth floor," the woman replied with confidence before excusing herself back into her office. "Enjoy!"

Josephine distractedly wandered the empty hallway of the fifth floor twice before concluding that she had been misled.

She hesitated a moment before knocking on a door on the fifth floor. This door was opened by a third bureaucrat: another polite young woman remarkable in her averageness. She assured Josephine that the vending machine was on the third floor. The skin around the woman's eyes was flushed, as though she had recently been crying, or maybe just rubbing her eyes too hard.

Josephine shivered several times as she reentered the elevator and descended to the third floor. Already the women's faces and forms were fading. Perhaps they hadn't resembled her so very much after all. But—hadn't they?

There she found it, at the far end of the hallway on the third floor. The vending machine was dusty with disuse. Most of the candy looked vintage, the bold colors and elaborate fonts of an earlier era. The rest of it looked brand-new, newer than new, candies she'd never heard of, futuristic white-and-silver packaging. She was grateful to recognize one item, the Mars bar—never her favorite but at least familiar. She slipped her quarters into the slot and punched the correct number. When she reached into the bin to retrieve the Mars bar, what she pulled out was a pack of lavender mints that looked like something her grandmother would have eaten as a child. She had no more quarters.

"Screw you," she whispered at the vending machine.

On her way up to the ninth floor in the elevator, she unwrapped the lavender candies. By the time she arrived back at her office, she was addicted to their perfumed taste, the sharp edges of each pale-purple square.

Halfway through the pack, her tongue started to bleed, cut by the candy as it disintegrated in her mouth, sharp as bird bones.

But all afternoon she kept eating lavender candies, inputting data, eating lavender candies, inputting data.

When she returned from work that day, he was pacing around the room. No candles, no dinner, just a brown-paper shopping bag under his arm.

"Let's go," he said before she was fully inside. "Put on something."

"Something?" she said. Her mouth was sore. She would never again eat another lavender candy.

"Festive," he said. "Suggestive. Progressive."

She wanted to scoff at that. Everything was in storage except for the meek clothing she wore to work. But she did put on a pair of oversize red plastic earrings.

They walked in the direction opposite the aboveground subway track and eventually came to the park. He led her around, searching for the perfect bench—near the lake, no gum gobs, not too close to an overflowing trash can. Several versions of the perfect bench were inhabited, so they settled for a less-than-perfect one, its paint peeling off in large patches. Still, they had a good view of the lake.

He pulled celebratory foods—a baguette and Brie, figs and olives and sparkling water and dark chocolate—out of the paper bag.

"What's the occasion?" she said.

"Life."

She tried to be delighted, but there was something peculiar about him. She bit into a fig, watched a pair of swans glide luminous in the transformative white light of sundown. One by one the pinkish lamps alongside the lake clicked on. The city was so generous sometimes. Here she could almost believe her windowless office in the gray building had ceased to exist. If no one is there to be mastered by the Database, is the Database still master?

"Aren't the swans nice?" she said.

"You mean the swan?" he said.

"There are two."

"One," he countered.

"Two!" she insisted.

She blinked at the swans. As she blinked, the double necks resolved themselves into a single neck.

"You're right," she admitted, irritated by her used-up eyes.

Two kids rolled shrieking down the little incline behind the bench, their skin golden and grass-marked in the lamplight, while the father egged them on and the mother looked upward and outward, away from her family.

"Crazy little zombie bambis," Joseph said. Sharply she looked over at him. She couldn't read his tone, irritated or charmed, weary or yearning.

Even after a night of figs and swans, her windowless office in AZ/ZA awaited her. But on Thursday morning she felt slightly calmer than usual, more open to speculation about the people represented by the files. A woman with a name like Esme Lafayette Gold had to have a more dramatic life than someone named Josephine Anne Newbury. She pictured metallic green eye shadow and satin dresses in gem hues and tragic loves, before chiding herself for falling into clichés; Esme could just as well be a first-grade teacher who always wore muted colors and went to bed at 8:30 p.m. Or maybe she was a first-grade teacher who wore metallic-green eye shadow. How about Jonathan Andrew Hall? Was he as bland and agreeable as his name suggested, or was he filled with rage? Did he go by JAH and listen to death metal? Had the very agreeableness of his name served as the seed of his rage?

She yawned and stretched her arms and looked at the ceiling, which had fewer marks and gashes than the walls. When she turned her attention back down to JAH's file, she screamed: The Person with Bad Breath was centimeters away from her desk.

"Goodness gracious," The Person with Bad Breath said, bringing hands to ears.

"Sorry, sorry, sorry!" Josephine said.

"Forgiven." The smile was dry, yes, but not unfriendly. "I trust that you are thriving here?"

She felt only somewhat deceitful as she nodded her agreement. The Person with Bad Breath didn't move to leave but instead seemed to be waiting for Josephine's next words.

"The work suits you, does it not?" The Person with Bad Breath said.

Emboldened by this note of kindness, by the slight vulnerability evident in the fact that her boss's shirt collar had flipped up in the back and was not lying impeccably beneath the gray jacket, Josephine found herself confessing: "I wonder about them."

"About whom?" The Person with Bad Breath inquired, as though it wasn't obvious. "Oh, *them*." Now moving toward the door, reaching for the knob, almost gone. "It is better never to wonder about them."

The orderly quiet of Josephine's office had alchemized into dense silence. She spent the rest of the workday blasting through files, devoid of curiosity, dying to get the hell home and just be a person with Joseph.

SIX

When she returned from work, he wasn't at the stranger's apartment. She pulled a postal notice off the door and stepped inside just as she heard the three-headed dog heave itself against the door at the end of the hall. Her hands felt weak and her eyes hazy. She added the postal notice to the stranger's feral pile of mail on the bedside table. She sat down on the futon. She called Joseph's phone. It went straight to voice mail. She didn't leave a message.

She opened the mini-fridge. There was half an onion and some expired sour cream. She was hungry and not hungry.

She decided to do good things. She lit the candles. She gathered up all the dirty laundry, sheets included, and tried to remember if the stranger had said anything about the location of the building's laundry room. But then she realized she had no quarters or detergent, and the thought of remedying those problems felt insurmountable. Anyway, they'd made it this far without doing laundry.

She found couscous and chickpeas in the cupboard. She found curry powder. She cut up the onion, turned on the burner, made something, ladled the concoction onto two of the stranger's green heirloom plates, spread the blanket on the floor, put a pair of candles in the middle, folded paper towels into napkins. She was pleased at her resourcefulness, notwithstanding her failure in regard to the laundry. She knew he would come in the door any second; every move she made, she imagined him walking in on that particular tableau, of her slicing or stirring or serving or folding, and she anticipated the exact expression he'd make, the thing with the eyebrows, the faux surprise, pretending he'd forgotten that she too could cook.

The food was cooling on the floor. She called his phone again; voice mail again. She turned on the radio balanced on the ledge in the stranger's shower stall and pretended the newsman's voice was Joseph talking to her from the other room, making measured and tranquilizing predictions about the future and the stock market. She waited, then devoured her food. She called him a third time and left a peevish voice mail. She texted him a single question mark.

Time passed; more than an hour. She called him again, told his voice mail that she was kind of freaking out. She vacillated between worry and rage. She couldn't stand to spend another second inside this apartment without him. There was a rotten smell emerging from the closet. For the first time it occurred to her to wonder if he'd left any sort of note. She shuffled through the stranger's unruly mail. The postal notice that had been on the door earlier slipped to the floor. She picked it up. She was about to stick it deep into the middle of the pile when the familiar letters caught her eye.

In the intended-recipient box: JOSEPHINE NEWBURY.

But they hadn't told anyone the address of the sublet.

She examined the notice. FIRST DELIVERY ATTEMPT FAILED: *Package could not be delivered/signature needed.* There was no information about the sender. Her fingers were quivering. She blew out the candles. She turned on the overhead light. A train ached past the window.

She now detested the automated lady who repeatedly offered her the option of leaving a voice message for Joseph Jones. Who, after many messages left, informed her that Joseph Jones's voice mailbox was full. She saw that her text had never been delivered. She considered calling the police. She imagined them laughing at her. A husband a few hours late getting home. Sorry, baby, you're not the first. The overhead light stared her down. She turned it off and sat awake on the bed for many hours.

SEVEN

At her desk on Friday, logging files into the Database, Josephine began to believe she was the only person in the entire building. It was so silent in 9997—no noise but the sound of her fingers on the keyboard, her fingers opening the files—that she sensed a scream beneath the silence, a shrill shriek she recognized as the flow of her own blood in her ears, yet it sounded like a banshee trapped in the walls. Those pinkish clawed walls—she generally avoided looking at them, but today she got stuck staring at the mysterious smudges and old fingerprints, as though the walls themselves might reveal his whereabouts.

Tonight she would call the police, and the parents, who had warned them what would happen if they left the hinterland. Her mother had stood in the beige kitchen of their hinterland rental, talking about the thing she'd seen on the news: Nowadays, gangs of teens in the big cities would just come up to strangers at random on the street and punch them. Just punch them in the face! As part of some gang initiation or something. And that was just the kind of horrid thing that happened in some places and not others. And what if, say, Josephine were to be pregnant at some point, and a gang of teens just punched her on the street? What then? Her mother knew exactly how to kill her every time. Her conversations with her mother were a list of things she thought but didn't say. Why would you move to a place where you don't know a living soul? (Haven't you noticed that our life here is not progressing, Mom? That we're stuck? That we're getting flattened by the freeways?) You'll be all alone there! (What about Joseph, Mom?) Friendless! (I'll be with Joseph, Mom. Love of my life, Mom.) But by then her mother was crying—melodramatic tears, yet still tears.

Friendless! Friendless! It lingered like a curse.

The door shot open. Josephine seized up, expecting The Person with Bad Breath, but it was Trishiffany who paraded in. She stood before Josephine's desk in a suit the color of a stop sign, hugging a single gray file to her breasts, her hair voluminous.

"Hi there, Jojo doll."

Josephine's gratitude at seeing another human being—wearing vivacious red, no less—was somewhat undercut by the inappropriate use of the nickname; her mother always insisted that everyone call her Josephine, and so they had. She opened the file at the top of the extra large crop on her desk (BRAAK/MARCUS/TODD) and tried to look busy.

"This is for you," Trishiffany announced, shoving her gray file atop BRAAK's.

OLGUIN/VIOLA/PINK. A unique enough name that Josephine remembered it, vaguely, from sometime last week.

"I already entered that one," Josephine said.

"Of course you did, Jojo doll," Trishiffany cooed, leaning over the desk almost seductively, revealing her cleavage. Josephine winced at the sight of the red capillaries in the whites of Trishiffany's eyes; her own eyes throbbed in solidarity. "But now you have to delete it."

"Delete it?" She turned her gaze away from Trishiffany's excessive chest and strained eyes. She was having trouble telling whether her coworker's tone was friendly or menacing.

"Well, just the date in the final column," Trishiffany clarified. She stood up straight, hands on hips, tapping her red high heel in a gesture typically associated with impatience, yet the gesture was contradicted by the patient smile on her face.

"I wasn't told that I'd ever be asked to delete anything," Josephine resisted.

Trishiffany sprang back and whipped out an ID card.

"I am your *super*ior," she said, thrusting the card at Josephine.

The ID meant nothing to Josephine, but official documents always made her nervous. That old anxiety of the DMV, the IRS.

Trishiffany smiled dazzlingly and came around to stand behind Josephine's chair.

"The Database is confidential," Josephine said, capitalizing the "D," trying to cover the spreadsheet with her hands, certain The Person with Bad Breath would appear at any instant.

"It's just a Processing Error," Trishiffany said; Josephine heard the capital "P" and "E." "I work in the Department of Processing Errors. I have clearance. I could read any file front to back any day of the week, J-doll."

"I made a processing error?" Josephine murmured. She had been so meticulous with the Database. She never wanted to return to those nineteen months of unemployment, that desperate feeling. She didn't need to understand her job; she just needed to keep it.

"Oh no Jojo," Trishiffany said, relishing the rhyme. She leaned voluptuously over the desk once more in a manner perhaps intended to be comforting. "It's a higher-up mistake. It happens. Please locate OLGUIN by her HS number."

Relieved, Josephine obeyed.

"There she is!" Trishiffany chortled. It was odd that she laughed. It didn't seem like the right time to laugh. "Go ahead and delete the date."

Josephine deleted it, one click, two clicks.

"Good girl!" Trishiffany said. "I'll take OLGUIN's file to Storage."

Josephine turned her attention back to BRAAK/MARCUS/TODD, hoping Trishiffany would leave. But instead she perched on the desk and examined the walls. Josephine typed BRAAK's HS number into the search function.

"These *walls*," Trishiffany groaned. "Are they driving you crazy yet?"

Josephine looked up. "Why doesn't someone repaint them?" she said.

"That work order was put in eight years ago, Jojo doll. They'll get around to it. But let's talk about something nice instead. How about your husband?"

Josephine stared darkly into the Database. Trishiffany didn't take the hint.

"Like, where did you meet him?" she persisted. "I want to meet a prince like him."

"College," Josephine said.

"Oh! Boohoo, too late for me." Trishiffany sighed. Then, rejuvenating herself: "When did you know you loved him?"

"I don't know," she said.

"You mean you don't know if you love him or you don't know when you knew you loved him?" Trishiffany demanded.

"Yes." She was unwilling to cooperate.

"Okay, fine then." Trishiffany eyed her. "What's he like?"

"Brown hair, brown eyes, average height." Josephine felt disinclined to elaborate, to explain that sometimes his hair seemed dark brown and sometimes light brown, that his eyes vacillated between coal and hazel, that he was tall when he stood up straight and short when he slouched, that he was at times lanky and at times stubby, that he could look like Dracula or like a woodsman, that once somebody had assumed he was Austrian, that another time a stranger had pegged him as Egyptian. How would she ever describe him to the police?

"Oh!" Trishiffany gasped. She was full of gasps and sighs. "I meant, you know, his personality."

Cynical, tender, thoughtful, realistic, pessimistic, calm, passive, anxious, eccentric, sensible, wry, courageous, clever, fidgety.

"I'm sorry," Josephine said. It was too hard to think about him. When she thought about him, her body got chaotic with panic. "I don't know how to describe him."

Trishiffany's made-up face drooped downward, and Josephine saw that she was crying.

"Your mascara," Josephine warned. She assumed runny mascara was the kind of thing that would scandalize a woman like Trishiffany. "Don't cry!" she added, trying not to let it sound like as urgent a plea as it was. She couldn't stand Trishiffany's inexplicable tears.

"I'm sorry, I'm sorry," Trishffany said. "It's just that I can see how much you love him. And it's so cute that you guys have the same name!" She catapulted herself off the desk and over to the door, where she paused. "They always drive the girls crazy but don't let them drive you crazy, okay?"

Young woman after young woman sitting at this same desk, listening to that same banshee silence, thinking about other lives—Josephine's neck tensed.

"They're just walls, after all," Trishiffany concluded.

Josephine was still trying to remember if she'd let Joseph's name drop when the door swung open again; Trishiffany had some final zinger.

But it was The Person with Bad Breath, reflective eyeglasses masking any expression.

"Hard at work," The Person with Bad Breath said. A command, not a question. Josephine could smell the breath from where she sat behind the desk—the mint veiled nothing.

EIGHT

S he didn't know whether to dawdle or rush on her way back to the stranger's apartment, and she ended up doing something in between, dashing ahead for a while and then hanging back. The three-headed dog was silent as she searched for the correct key. Before she'd inserted the key, the door opened.

Joseph held a large red fruit in his right hand.

"You!" she said, furious and overjoyed.

He pulled her into the room and double-locked the door behind her. Then he handed her the fruit.

"What's this?" she said.

"A pomegranate." He sounded tired. But also, maybe, elated. That note of elation or whatever it was—it made her uneasy.

"Where the hell were you?" she said, wishing she were the kind of person who could recognize a pomegranate when she saw it.

"Working," he said. "It was urgent."

"You didn't call."

"It was urgent," he repeated. "An emergency."

"I thought your job was boring."

"There was a deadline."

"You should have called."

He cupped her neck with both hands and smiled at her, a frank smile, his eyes direct into hers. His irises were nearly black.

"You should have called."

He nodded.

An ice cream truck passed down below, its gleeful tune crackling through a malfunctioning speaker.

"If you ever do that again," she threatened.

But he was already heading into the kitchenette to fry four eggs in lots of butter.

He flipped the eggs with his typical ease, yet she noted certain things—the swift rhythm his fingers tapped on the spatula, the shakiness of the water glass in his hand.

She didn't want to speculate. It was hard not to speculate.

"Did you—" she said.

"Grab me the pepper?" he said.

She passed him the salt, the pepper, the plates.

They sat cross-legged on the floor in the candlelight, their knees touching. He told her about the new sublet he'd found for them—a garden apartment not far from here, on the same subway line, a tad farther from downtown but nicer than this place.

And soon their credit would be restored and they could get their own place and start the different kind of life anew.

"Hug me," she said when they were done eating. She could hear that she sounded whiny, like a small child. But he owed it to her.

Joseph set their plates aside. He hugged her. It was awkward to hug sitting up so they lay down on the blanket on the floor.

There had been moments, last night, when she had imagined him never returning: life without Joseph. Recalling that abandoned, bereft version of herself, she pressed her hip bones against his hip bones. She felt him respond to the pressure of her and it made her proud.

"Hello," she said.

"Hello," he said.

She unsnapped her skirt and squirmed out of it.

"I don't know," he said, sitting up.

"Excuse me?" she said, also sitting up. She pointed at his cock, thick and solid inside his pants.

He started to say something and then stopped. He looked at the ceiling and then at her. Tonight his hair was dark and sharp, like a demon's.

"Maybe we should," he paused, "wait."

She was enraged. Suspicion swelled inside her.

"What's wrong with you?" she said ferociously.

"Okay, okay, okay, okay, okay," he said. He lay back down, pulling her with him. He unbuttoned his shirt. He unzipped his pants. She watched him until he was naked except for his socks.

"Socks too," she insisted.

He obeyed.

Then he reached for her shirt, pulled it over her head. He helped with her tights, her underwear, navigating them over her feet. She got on top of him. It was a relief to be so close. She found herself relaxing, moving in the familiar way.

"Did you hear something?" he said after a moment. His voice was curt, cutting through the candlelight.

"Something?" she said. She was all dreamy now and she didn't like the way he was softening inside her.

"Someone? In the hallway?"

"I don't know. Maybe. That dog." She was moving her hips around him in a circle. She didn't want to worry about whatever it was that he was worrying about.

She felt like he was trying to not come. There was resistance in his muscles. It made her angry and she pressed harder and moved faster. She put her mouth very close to his mouth and when he cried out the sound was inside her skull too. She scooted up to his mouth and knelt above him and then when he made her come she fell forward onto her hands, laughing.

"041-74-3400!" she said.

It was time to cut the pomegranate.

"I'll do it," she insisted, even though she had no idea how to do it.

She pulled down one of the stranger's heirloom plates, balanced it on the narrow strip of countertop, jabbed at the pomegranate with a steak knife. Thick red blobs of liquid shot out of the fruit, spraying the wall and the cabinets. The plate flipped off the countertop and shattered on the linoleum floor.

Joseph and Josephine stood guiltily on the sidewalk beneath the streetlight in the slight rain, surrounded by overstuffed suitcases and canvas bags brimming with uneasy contents. A mostly drunk bottle of cheap white wine poked out amid stale laundry. Their umbrella was broken, its elbows splayed like a bad joke. It was desolate beneath the train tracks. No cab came along. Then a cab

came along, but its driver sped up when he saw them. They waited
a very long time. In the building behind them, the three-headed
dog stirred, as dark and frenetic as ever, and a fake heirloom plate
charaded among the other three.

The cabdriver who finally picked them up told them all about
the faraway farm he owned; he raised cows and grew bananas on
another continent, and soon he would return to that place to live
forever. Josephine felt ill with envy, but still she politely inquired
about growing practices for tropical fruits.

Instead of a garden, the garden apartment possessed a dim
entryway that smelled like a cellar. There wasn't even a flower-
pot. There was, however, as Joseph pointed out, a butterfly quilt
on the bed.

"And the bathtub is pink," he announced from the bathroom.

She felt bad that he felt bad for not knowing that "garden" was
a code word for "basement" in housing ads here.

"I'll take a bath," she said, trying to be okay with things. But
when she went to draw water, black gunk bubbled up from the
drain. She gagged and ran to him in the kitchen.

"It's just a baby," he said.

She was confused for a moment, until she noticed a small
cockroach plodding toward the fridge.

"I just want to feel immaculate for a few minutes a day," she
said.

Walking outside in the sun made Josephine feel immaculate.
Peppermint ice cream and sleeping for eight hours and not having to touch any gray files and giving dollar bills to subway vio-
linists and drinking big glasses of water and buying a 50% off
wall calendar of nature scenes from the hinterland. Joseph did
what he could, though the weekend was often overcast. And
though he had always been a fidgeter, though his fidgeting had

been a decade-long irritant to Josephine, it had escalated to a ter-rific new level.

"What's wrong with you, 041-74-3400?" she finally said on Sunday afternoon as he fiddled simultaneously with the table leg, the saltshaker, and a spoon.

"I'm scared," he confessed.

Sympathy flooded her. She seized the saltshaker and the spoon. She knew with sudden, cool certainty that he would never again abandon her; that she would never again sit through a night alone wondering where he was. At least not until he died.

"Join the club," she said.

"Loin the lub," he replied.

NINE

On Monday morning, she tacked the new calendar—color photographs of fields of wildflowers—to the wall beside her desk. It hid some of the smudges. She'd resisted looking ahead to the next month's image, so now she could spend the rest of this month in a state of minor anticipation.

But for now, Monday: One's entire mind had to report for duty, for cross-checking.

Names swelled and ebbed beneath her fingertips. She began to forget they represented flesh and blood. Instead, it became a kind of game, the search for funny names, names that sounded as if children had made them up, any scrap of entertainment amid the endless and endlessly average names: IDA ABAGABA, TIMOTHY BONEBREAK, SADIE ELBOW. She still got a little thrill from noticing the coincidences—eighteen "F" surnames in a row, three with the middle name Eve, a SARAH JANE followed immediately by a SARAH JEAN.

Bolstered by the relative peace of the weekend, she discovered a pocket of cheerfulness inside herself, a newfound gratitude for her situation. Joseph was back and well; here she sat at this desk like the captain of a tiny ship; she knew what to do and how to do it; she was well hydrated. Tonight, after completing her allotted tasks in a methodical fashion, she would go home to him. The money was mounting in their little bank account, which had hovered right around zero for so many months. This was a life; it was a life; it was her life. These tranquilizing thoughts carried her through the day until midafternoon, when she glanced up to find The Person with Bad Breath standing quietly in her doorway. She tried to hide her startled shiver.

"Oh dear," The Person with Bad Breath said, pointing a grayish finger at the calendar. "You mustn't hang anything on the walls. Otherwise the painters might get discouraged when they come."

"Okay," Josephine said.

The Person with Bad Breath waited.

Josephine yanked the tack out of the wall. The calendar fell to the floor. Bending to pick it up, she saw old strands of hair and clumps of dust beneath her desk, decades' worth of mustiness.

"Thatta girl," The Person with Bad Breath said, but in that arid mouth, the colloquialism sounded wrong.

"Wasn't the work order for the walls put in eight years ago?" Josephine muttered when the door was mostly shut. She spent half a minute hoping she hadn't been heard, and the next half minute hoping she had.

She kicked at the stubborn bottom drawer of her desk, tugged it open, and slid the offending calendar in. She was about to slam the drawer shut when she paused, retrieved the calendar, reopened it to the correct month: a sloping alpine hillside covered in yellow and purple flowers. As foreign to her now in this room as a picture of another planet in another galaxy. She stroked the gleaming page. She narrowed her eyes at it, tried to see into the forest beyond the meadow; was there a woman, a woman carrying a child on her back, standing among the shadows of the pine trees? The glare of the fluorescent light on the glossy page obscured the image, and her eyes were weak from hours of work.

She clutched the tack, pierced the wall, hung the calendar right back up where it had been.

It lightened her step, that minuscule act of defiance, on her walk from the subway back to the so-called garden apartment that night. She passed a take-out Chinese restaurant, stopped to look through the big window at the illuminated menu, contemplated the oddly appealing possibility of oversweet sesame chicken, felt somewhat hopeful.

But then she noticed a man in jeans and a gray sweatshirt standing inside the restaurant—his skin ill against the pale green walls—staring hard at her. There was an eerie focus in his eyes, as if he'd singled her out. Or he could have just been gazing vacantly out the window.

Unnerved, Josephine hurried onward. As soon as she began to walk away, the man in the gray sweatshirt headed briskly toward the door of the restaurant. She sped up, running the final blocks, unwilling to look back to confirm that he was following her, worried that a backward glance might provoke him. Only once she had reached the dubious safety of the dark stairwell did she dare a glance. The sidewalk behind her was empty.

She smiled a thin, scornful smile at her nervous little self. Still, it was a relief to stumble down the cellar steps, to throw her bag on the rickety chair and call out for Joseph.

He wasn't there. She almost enjoyed her slight buzz of impatience, of doubt; when he arrived, any moment now, she wouldn't take him for granted; "041-74-3400!" she'd say.

His phone went straight to voice mail. His voice mailbox was full. She had just hung up when a text message dinged. She seized her phone, but the text was from her mother: *Apples in season went to orchard today you should be here. Pie!*

She sat at the kitchen table. The basement was all shadows and earth smells. At least there were no cockroaches in sight. She crept through the rooms. Even the most innocuous objects had taken on an undeniable malevolence—the rag rug, the plastic trash can, the butterfly quilt. She returned to the kitchen. She drank a glass of water. She felt unwell. She was just transitioning into fury when her phone began to buzz on the table.

"Where are you?" she demanded.

The brief reply was a blur of indecipherable noise.

"Where are you?" she screamed.

This time the response was a mangled mutter. Maybe a trio of gerunds (*doing gluing screwing*) or maybe not. Distorted syllables, and then, clear as anything, an exhausted sigh before his voice sank back into the muck of static.

"I can't hear you!" She could hear how savage she sounded.

He launched into a bunch of words but she only caught fragments, blips and fuzz.

". . . sticksorhoe . . . portentgif . . . nessandheal . . . ed . . . oon . . ."

"What?" she shrieked.

He said something that seemed to end with an exclamation. *"What?"*

". . . so that—" Joseph's voice emerged loud and perfectly distinct for two words, followed by the total silence of a lost connection.

TEN

The Four-Star Diner was packed with its Monday-night dinner crowd, but even so Hillary hustled over the second Josephine stepped through the doorway. Her orange ponytail was brighter than anything else in that bright place.

"There you are!" Hillary bellowed. "Right this way, sugar-plum." She put an arm around Josephine and bustled her toward the row of red stools by the counter. She looked older than Josephine remembered. "What'll it be? Tuna melt? Grilled cheese? Wait, no, breakfast for dinner—how about waffles? Pancakes? Strawberries, right? Bingo! Lady in need of strawberry pancakes! Listen, I'll be right back, I've got a table of grannies that wants a million things."

Hillary delivered the food quickly, with a wink, and Josephine ate quickly, almost rudely, the way Joseph always ate. The instant the pancakes were gone, she once again had that feeling of not knowing what to do with herself; the long fast walk to the diner had been something to do, eating had been something to do, but now the grief was beating the frenzy, the fury. Hillary came by to wipe down the counter.

"So, tell me," she said to Josephine as if they were best friends. "Where'd he go?"

Josephine focused on the saltshaker.

"Oh honey," Hillary said. "You look just terrible! I knew it the second you walked in the door. Actually, I knew it the second you kids spent the night here back whenever it was. I told you I'm a psychic, right? Hang around till things quiet down, okay?"

Josephine rested her forehead against her fingertips, felt the Braille of her rising zits. She drank a few of the mini-creams, flinging them down her throat like shots. The dinner crowd thinned. She watched a large family group clogging the exit, the merry chaos as they located the grandfather's coat, the baby's pacifier. Idly, distantly, she wondered if she'd ever typed any of their names into the Database.

She was still entranced by the baby, who had violent hiccups and messy curls, when someone gripped her hand and flipped it upward on the paper place mat. Josephine twisted around to find Hillary leaning over the counter, already deep in the study of her palm. The smell of cigarettes and Dove soap and syrup. The sleeves of her royal-purple uniform were rolled up, showing off the green snake on her forearm. Her hand was warm, almost hot, and muscular, and enviably dry; Josephine's palms were always clammy. Though it was awkward, her fingers pinned down this way by a near-stranger, she couldn't deny that Hillary's touch felt as good as someone brushing your hair, someone massaging your shoulders.

"You have a lot of unused capacity that you haven't turned to your advantage," Hillary murmured, squinting at the lines. "Disciplined and self-controlled outside, you tend to be worrisome and insecure inside."

Josephine tried to pull her hand away, but Hillary wouldn't let go.

"You're critical of yourself," she persisted. "At times you have serious doubts about whether you've made the right decision or done the right thing."

Josephine put her free hand up to her neck, attempted to locate the knot in her throat.

"You've found it unwise to be too frank in revealing yourself to others," Hillary said slowly. "You pride yourself on being an independent thinker. You're often introverted, wary, and reserved. Still, you frequently desire the company of others. Security is one of your major goals in life, but you become dissatisfied when hemmed in. Some of your aspirations are unrealistic."

Hillary stopped, noticing the effect of her words, and pulled a napkin from the metal dispenser, placed it in Josephine's exposed palm.

"Don't worry," she said, "it's normal to cry. Everyone does."

Josephine felt naked, ashamed, far too understood. She swiped the napkin across her face and stared at the unfair red hair. Was Hillary kind or cruel?

"I'm just the messenger, sugarplum," Hillary said. "Are you ready for the good news?"

Josephine spread her hand out on the countertop again, but Hillary ignored it.

"Though you have some personality weaknesses, you're generally able to compensate for them," she announced.

Josephine waited. Hillary smiled.

"That's all?" Josephine said.

"That's plenty," Hillary said.

"Where is he? When will he come back? Will we stay married? Will we have kids? How many? How long will I live?"

"Oh sugarplum," Hillary chided. "You don't want to know any of that."

"Yes I *do!*" Josephine was alarmed by the screech in her own voice.

"Want a refill on that coffee?" Hillary said, standing up straight again and offering Josephine the dazzling, indifferent smile of any great diner waitress. She glided away as though nothing significant had passed between them.

Josephine left a huge tip, wound her scarf around her neck as many times as possible, and stepped from the pink and yellow glow of the diner out into the night, dead leaves racing down the concrete all around her.

"Don't worry so much, sugarplum!" She thought she'd escaped unnoticed, but Hillary tossed out the penny-bright words before the door blew shut. "It's bad for your skin!"

ELEVEN

There was a soft knock on the door of Josephine's office, followed by a hard shove, and in came Trishiffany, wearing a pink ball gown so wide she got stuck in the doorway, but she hardly seemed to notice. She worked a gob of gum on her tongue into an enormous bubble. As the bubble grew, it began to resemble some unidentifiable body part, a kidney or a liver or a uterus, something dark pink and veiny. When the bubble popped, bits of the organ flew back onto Trishiffany's face and melted down her ball gown. Trishiffany giggled. Something was pushing her from behind, pressing her forward, and when she and her ball gown finally surged into the office, Josephine saw that the force behind Trishiffany was Joseph.

In the morning, Josephine's eyes were bloodshot. The drain in the pink bathtub was still malfunctioning, bubbling blackness. She scrubbed her armpits with a washcloth over the sink and gave her face a brief splash. The artificial light accentuated the tense tendons in her neck. She felt scared of herself. Her fingers were unreliable; she lost her grip, dropped her toothbrush. Joseph's voice mail was still full.

She got dressed for work, drank a glass of water, tried to cool her panic with ten deep breaths—*disciplined and self-controlled outside, you tend to be worrisome and insecure inside*—before stepping into what proved to be a brisk, merciful September morning. She stood in the doorway for a moment, looking upward out of the stairwell at all the leaves on the brink of yellow, before spotting the postal notice on the door.

JOSEPHINE NEWBURY. SECOND DELIVERY ATTEMPT FAILED.

They hadn't shared this new temporary address with anyone either. The minuscule comfort offered by the brightness of the day vanished.

Back in the office with the wounded walls, Josephine concluded that there *was* a woman carrying a child, the pair almost entirely obscured by trees and shadows beyond the field of alpine flowers. Unless it was just her imagination. Still, the possibility soothed her. But, despite the columbines, she kept finding herself stuck in a blank stare on Tuesday. She would realize she had gone whole minutes looking at a bruise on the wall above the calendar. She tried to amend this, tried to look at the world with precision, but eventually she had to admit that she couldn't avoid or control it, couldn't escape it. Squiggly lines writhed across her vision.

When a headache blossomed outward from deep within her skull, she scurried to the bathroom. She attempted to evade her own blank stare in the mirror by focusing on the intricate pattern of capillaries in her eyes, miniature red wires going in one side of her iris and coming out the other. She pitied her eyes as though they were delicate, abused animals that didn't belong to her. Her skin was taking on the same sallow pinkish color as the walls of her office. She counted five zits risen on her forehead.

The bathroom door opened; Josephine froze, as though she'd been caught.

"Jojo doll!" Today her suit was orange with yellow piping. "Hangin' in there?"

"Hi," Josephine whispered, darting past Trishiffany and out the door. It wasn't that she didn't want to talk to Trishiffany; today of all days she wanted to talk to her, to talk to someone, anyone, to say out loud, I am so sad, to rattle off a list of suspicions. *You frequently desire the company of others.* But just the sight of her—her friendly question, her bright clothing—uncapped a roar of fear inside Josephine's head, as though all her defenses would disintegrate at the slightest indication of a kind listener. *You've found it unwise to be too frank in revealing yourself to others.* It had never occurred to her that something aside from death might separate her from Joseph.

She spent the rest of the day working as diligently as a robot. A dutiful, mechanical heart.

The door of The Person with Bad Breath's office was always closed, but today, as Josephine was leaving at five, it happened to be propped open. Through the crack, she glimpsed her boss talking on the telephone, feet propped up on the metal desk, argyled ankles precisely crossed.

"HS129285656855," The Person with Bad Breath was saying

in a bored, irritable voice. "One—Two—Nine—Two—Eight—Five—Six—Five—*Six—Eight—Five—Five.*"

Overwhelmed by dread, Josephine rushed faster than usual to exit the building.

She stood in the doorway of the cellar apartment and said his name seven times before accepting that he wasn't there.

She closed the door behind her. Stood perfectly still in the entryway. She had no idea at all what to do with the next minutes of her life. It was best and easiest to stop here, not move another inch. Not think about who to call or what to report. She would have stood there forever, just blinking and breathing, except that soon she became desperate to pee.

She ran down the unlit hall to the bathroom, swearing to herself that as soon as she was done she'd come right back to the entryway, stand there still. She peed in the dark, wiped in the dark, flushed in the dark. On her way back to her post, she spotted something in the bedroom: a long black shape on the bed.

She thought it was an intruder before she thought it could be him.

Naked, and sleeping on his side, as he always did.

Her life had become so odd.

She shrugged off her cardigan, stepped out of her shoes. She lay down on the butterfly quilt behind him and cupped his body with hers, as she always did. A few minutes of stillness.

Sometime soon, sometime very soon, she would let go of him, would wake him up to demand explanations, pretending she'd never held him at all.

When she lifted her arm off him in preparation for the fight, he grabbed her wrist. She gasped, startled—he had seemed so dead asleep.

"Don't go," he said, pivoting around to grab her other wrist.

"Ha," she said coldly.

He sat up, her wrists still locked in his fingers. His skin looked strange, evil, gleaming nude in the pale alley light that snuck down the window well.

She was having trouble recognizing him. He seemed euphoric, rich with energy, almost superhuman.

"Are you a demon?" she said.

"Demon demeanor," he said. "Demoner."

He dropped her wrists and went for the buttons on her blouse. She slapped his hands hard, as hard as she could; it felt good.

"Demean or?" she spat.

"Nice," he said, reaching once more for her buttons. "More, please."

She obliged with another slap.

"Take your clothes off," he commanded like a rapist. "It's important."

"You sound like a rapist," she said.

He laughed like a rapist. "You were the one who wanted it last time."

"I wouldn't have sex with you now for—" she failed.

"For what?" He was abuzz, brimming over, unable to cap his vitality.

"A million dollars!" she raged, clichéd. "All the tea in China!"

"But you have to," he said, jubilant. His hands firm again on her wrists. He was naked and she was dressed but they both knew who was really naked and who was really dressed.

She couldn't understand anything anymore. What was happening to him? Was their life together almost over? *Some of your aspirations are unrealistic.* He was touching her hand. Maniacally stroking the lines of her palm. It reminded her of something. She pulled her hand away. She curled herself around herself.

"Everything is good," he said.

She wished to make herself into a perfect sphere, no handles for him to grip.

"If you understood you'd understand," he said. "Take off your clothes."

She made a sound of protest.

"Think of it as make-up sex," he suggested.

"What about the fight?" she said to her knees.

"I'm sorry," he said, "and I'm not sorry."

He grabbed her, the ball of her, and peeled her arms from her legs.

She was fierce; she clung to herself; he laughed as though it was a game; maybe it was a game; she swatted at him, she twisted her spine, she pretended to be air but always he got hold of a limb.

She gave up. Lay flat on her back on the butterfly quilt. He trailed his lips down her chin, down her neck, all the way down. That infuriating mix of wrath and desire.

Later, she was above him, eyes shut, pressing her hands against the dust-thickened window, taking those long deep insane light-headed breaths that come just before, and then, as it hit, she opened her eyes with a scream of joy—there on the other side of the dim window was a man, a trespasser, his splayed fingers an echo of her splayed fingers, his oily face lengthened in an expression of ecstasy, his eyes brilliant gray and wide open. Her scream of joy veered into a scream of horror; her eyes snapped shut for safety.

Joseph rose up from beneath her, puzzled, normal, saying the right comforting things, asking the right concerned questions.

When she opened her eyes again, the window was empty, the maniac vanished. She pulled Joseph back down so they were both low on the bed, hidden. Mistaking her urgency for desire, he pushed himself into her again, and who was she to deny the heft of it, the absoluteness of his presence, the seam ripping beneath them.

TWELVE

Every morning the Database awaited her like a living thing, luminous and familiar, alongside stacks of gray files. It was wise to put bureaucrats in windowless offices; had there been a window, September might have taunted her with its high and mighty goldenness. As it was, she and the files were headed into the murky depths of Friday. Her blank stare frequently resurfaced, positively vengeful, separating her from the world with its indifferent glaze. The files mocked her, their voices whispery as paper cuts. She worked coldly, like someone who had never loved—there was ice inside her, notwithstanding the past two days, during which Joseph had made her hot chocolate with five spices each night, delivered in a large mug along with whipped cream and a series of reassurances, received with a roll of her bloodshot eyes.

At noon she sat at her desk, in the clawed pinkish cube that had become her life, eating a cheese-and-mustard sandwich. The sandwich was soggy, falling apart, virtually inedible, yet she never let things go to waste. The lonesomeness of the bureaucrat's lunch.

But then there was Trishiffany, appearing almost magically in her bubble-gum suit, slamming the door shut behind her, placing a plate of cookies covered in pink plastic wrap on Josephine's desk.

"For me?" Josephine said shyly, like a starlet winning an award.

"Anything for you, Jojo doll!" Trishiffany said. "Hey, I'm your best friend here, aren't I?"

There was, of course, little to no competition (Josephine remembered with slight yearning the three busy lookalike bureaucrats who had [mis]directed her to the vending machine). Still, that didn't take away from the extreme tenderness she suddenly discovered in herself toward Trishiffany, who was busily unwrapping the plastic and pushing the plate toward her.

"Kitchen-sink cookies," Trishiffany proclaimed. "Sounds disgusting, right? But I've always been so torn about chocolate chips versus butterscotch chips, but here you don't even have to choose! Walnuts *and* peanuts! Oatmeal *and* cornflakes! Raisins *and* dried cherries! Not to mention the shredded coconut. Sometimes we just need our freedom, you know?"

The cookies were fat and dense and golden. Trishiffany watched her pick one up.

"So?" Trishiffany demanded before her victim had finished the first bite.

Josephine had something to say but she hesitated to say it.

"*So?*" Trishiffany repeated.

"This is the food I've always wanted to eat," she confessed.

"Of course!" Trishiffany purred. "Of course it is, Jojo doll."

Josephine finished the cookie and began another. But Trishiffany wasn't eating.

"What, making me eat alone?" Josephine said.

"Oh . . . my girlish figure." Trishiffany looked down at the pink lines of her hips.

"What about *my* girlish figure?" she retorted, picking up a third cookie, and then paused, wondering if the cookies might be poisoned.

"Well I haven't been through what you've been through lately," Trishiffany said. "You've earned a cookie or seven."

"What I've been through lately?" Josephine repeated slowly, alarmed. She hadn't said a word to anyone about anything. Yet at the same time it felt so pleasant to hear someone express compassion for her situation. But then she conjectured, with a jolt, that Trishiffany could be the other woman. "What have I been through lately?" she said, guarded, testing the waters.

"Oh Jojo doll!" Trishiffany said. "You're so cute! You don't need to be so suspicious all the time, you know?"

Josephine looked directly into Trishiffany's bloodshot eyes. Her own tired eyes recognized themselves in her coworker's. *You tend to be worrisome and insecure inside.* She dismissed her ludicrous hunch.

"I know," Josephine admitted. She bit into the third cookie. The cork was loosening—she wanted to talk to Trishiffany—about her bad skin, her unreliable eyes, her vanishing husband, the man in the Chinese restaurant, the vagabond in her orgasm. She wanted to be held by someone kind. She wanted to cry into a cocktail across from a woman who always remembered Kleenex in her purse.

Trishiffany blinked, then winked. "Let me know if you ever need a free hug," she said. "I'm all about the free hug, you know? The other day I saw a guy on the subway holding a sign that said FREE HUG, and I was all about that."

At that, Josephine (*introverted, wary, reserved*) retreated into herself, denied herself. She barely knew a thing about Trishiffany, after all.

"Thanks for the offer," she said politely. "I'll let you know, if/when."

For the first time since Josephine had met her, Trishiffany looked uncomfortable—maybe that was even a slight blush beneath her blush.

"So, do you—have a boyfriend or anything?" Josephine attempted, wanting to change the subject, extend an olive branch. She'd gotten so rusty at friendship since they left the hinterland, where she had a handful of girlfriends, all of whom were far more talkative and confessional than she'd ever felt comfortable being with them.

It was easy to imagine Trishiffany in a kitchen, baking something full of butter and sugar for a man who found her delightful. It was easy to picture her someday soon soothing an infant with those huge breasts.

"No," Trishiffany said flatly, all the bubbles in her voice popped.

An awful misstep. To make a nice person like Trishiffany feel bad about having nobody. She really was a nice person, never mind certain irritating traits. Josephine hesitated, unsure whether or not she should apologize.

"I'm all about living vicariously!" Trishiffany rebounded. "Don't worry about me, Jojo doll. I've got everything I need, you know? One does what one has to do for oneself. Enjoy those cookies, okay?"

"You're too kind," Josephine said. She meant it so much that she choked up on the "k."

"Least I can do," Trishiffany said with a final wink.

Nobody.

No body.

Oneself.

One's elf.

"Hello?" Josephine said into the solitude of her office. It felt as though someone had spoken. She looked at the Database. She looked at the files. She looked at the injured walls.

Eel ho.

She couldn't cap the laugh that popped out of her. Immediately afterward she felt like a crazy lady.

Crazy lazy.

Hazy dazy.

"Hello?" she said again.

Eel ho.

At 4:57 p.m., The Person with Bad Breath opened the door and deposited a box of gray files on Josephine's desk.

"Fifty-six for immediate processing," The Person with Bad Breath announced. The breath mint tried and failed. The face seemed even more undefined than usual.

Josephine wished she were brave enough to say that it was a Friday, that she absolutely had to leave in three minutes. Instead, she nodded mildly and pulled the first file out of the box. Wasn't there a fairy tale about a girl with a spindle and a room of infinite straw?

In order to make her task somewhat less unbearable, she imagined the people represented by the files, pictured them in various states of animation—a pair of eyes squinting, a hand selecting fruit in a grocery store, a body passing through a doorway. She entertained herself with the fantasy of meeting them—at, say, a bar with wooden walls, tin ceilings, bottles of glowing bronze liquids. She envisioned them rising up from behind the bars of the Database, stepping into her life, shaking her hand, ordering their drinks of choice, getting a little tipsy, slinging their arms over her shoulders, bestowing damp kisses upon her forehead, thanking her for her service.

Yet that fantasy could only last so long; eventually, exhausted, she gave in to the relentlessness of typing 09272013 fifty-six times, didn't even search for coincidences, let the letters be nothing more than letters, the numbers nothing more than numbers. FASAD/ FADIL/MURR . . . FISHBEIN/SAMUEL/BLAKE . . . HOLGATE/CATHERINE/ JOAN . . . KAPLOWITZ/MICHAEL/EPHRON . . . LAZAN-VINCENT/PAU- LINA/RENEE . . . MCGOWAIN/THERESE/RAINE . . . MCMURPHY/SHAN- NON/SIOBHAN . . . MURCER/JONATHAN/KEITH . . . PANIAGUA/YASMIN/ JADE . . . PRINCE/JOSHUA/DAVID . . . SCANDURA/DAVID/SCOTT . . . SCHMIDT/DIANE/HOPE . . . SHAFIQ/IMRAN/SEAN . . . SMITH/LYNETTE/ ARLENE . . . TOUSSAINT/PAOLO/IVES . . . TROILER/JENNIFER/ BROWN . . . YAU/TZER/SUNG . . . ZILBERMAN/EZRA/TODD . . .

THIRTEEN

On Sunday morning her eyes were still bloodshot, stained from the week. Her stomach awoke her, angry with emptiness. It was easier now than it used to be to disentangle herself from the heat of his sleep, abandon him in the bed. All these years she'd disliked that moment each morning when he or she first got out of bed, leaving the other; today she almost relished it, separating her body from his.

Lick our.

Lick or rich.

It was licorice she wanted, licorice she needed: licorice black enough to turn her insides green.

Not even the dirty bar of blue soap in the bathroom or the baby cockroach meandering down the counter could dull her desire. She brushed her teeth, drank a glass of water, noticed a stain on the low ceiling.

She used to always leave a note, but not anymore. "041-74-3400?" she whispered into the bedroom as she buttoned her sweater.

Outside, the gray light flattened everything to gray.

A pair of rats zigzagged across the subway tracks. They looked scared, searching for something down there. They made her tired. He was moved by subway rats. "They're cute," he had countered in their early days here, when she complained about the vermin in the subway, the savagery of this city.

Save age.

Savant airy.

"Hello?" she muttered.

Eel ho.

The train appeared, pressing a stagnant wind before it, arriving with a series of weary shrieks.

The candy store was closed. It was 7:43 a.m. on a Sunday morning. The store would open in three hours and seventeen minutes. *Some of your aspirations are unrealistic.* She stood before the window, ravenous. There was an enormous glass jar of black licorice on display. She looked at herself in the jar until she felt as though the licorice were part of her face. Her skin buzzed.

Eventually she broke her own stare, returned to the world of the sidewalk, the very occasional pedestrians, a man in a gray sweatshirt passing behind her.

Back on the subway train, an elegant beggar—long white hair, loose dusty suit—listed foods as he limped down the car. "Egg sandwich. Spaghetti. Falafel." He held out a paper cup and shook

it to the rhythm of his words. A string of snot stretched downward from his nose onto his shirt, gracefully holding its slim shape
for six inches or more. "Cheddar cheese. Tacos. Toast with grape
jam. A chocolate milk shake."

He repulsed her, made her hungrier than ever, and she turned,
looked out the window into the darkness. The walls of the subway tunnel glistened with some kind of moisture.

"Skittles! M&M's! Snickers!" the beggar begged. "Black licorice!"

She whipped back around to look at him, certain he would
be staring at her, into her. But he was already pressing through
the interior doors, shuffling into the next car.

There was a Sunday-morning newspaper abandoned on the
seat beside her. Usually she wouldn't touch a stray item on
the subway, but she felt uneasy, desirous of distraction.

NEWLYWEDS, CHEF, ENGINEER AMONG PLANE CRASH VICTIMS . . .
Late Friday night, just off the coast . . . Only a limited number of
the victims' names have been released: Marvin Anderson (43), Hil-
ary Bower (35), Jerome Chavez (67), Jillian Coleman (52), Alison
Egret (27), Sam Fishbein (31).

Sam Fishbein.
Sam Fishbein.
FISHBEIN/SAMUEL/BLAKE
At this time, an estimated fifty-six fatalities.

"What happened to your fingers?" he said when she stumbled
through the door of the cellar. He was making oatmeal. "You like
it with cinnamon, right?"

She looked down. Her fingers were gray, deadened, and it took
her a long moment to realize that the newsprint had rubbed off
onto her skin.

FOURTEEN

Early Monday morning, Josephine scurried down the long hallway, covering her ears with her hands. Only now did she recognize that over the past few weeks she'd grown deaf to the typewriters' drone, but today she could hear it again, unbearably, the quiet roar of a million cockroaches marching. It was early—but not early enough to beat the typists.

"What's wrong with the clock?" he had said from the bed after she rose in the half dark. He was disoriented, dreaming.

"Don't worry, don't worry," she'd whispered until he put his head back down on the pillow. "I've got to go in early today."

"Is there a dog?" he murmured from beneath the butterfly quilt.

Now she darted into the dubious sanctuary of her office, where six high stacks of gray files awaited her, the weekend backlog.

Perhaps she worked for an airline.

She sat down. She opened the top file of the first stack. AMATTO/ ANNA/MARLENA. She slammed it shut.

She did not pick up the next file. She did not put her fingers on the keyboard. She stood up. She sat down.

The Database hummed, hungry.

She opened and then immediately closed the top file of the second stack (EATHER/HARVEY/JAMES), the fifth stack (PESAVENTO/ ARTURO/BENJAMIN).

What was she going to do. Was she going to sit here all day trembling, opening and closing files, ignoring the Database.

She reopened PESAVENTO/ARTURO/BENJAMIN. D09302013. Today's date.

But if her theory was correct, "D" didn't stand for "date."

For the first time, she scrutinized the second line of the form. She'd seen it before, of course, thousands of times, but always just as a dense blur of typewritten letters and numbers.

G1(Z)01102003G2(B)01152003G3(E)01252003G4(F)31220 03G10052003

She could see now, through her shame, that they were dates, the numbers lodged between the letters; she was stupid not to have noticed this before.

Understanding rushed through her, around her, enveloping her, suffocating her. She would prefer not to do this. She did not want to think along these lines. But, working backward, looking at line two (confused, still, by the puzzling letters throughout the row), couldn't she perhaps guess that all those 2003 dates bore some essential relationship to the D09302013, notwithstanding the "G" where she might have expected a "B"?

But no. It wasn't possible. If she happened to be correct, that meant that today a ten-year-old boy named Arturo Benjamin Pesavento—

Art jam save.

"Excuse me?" Josephine whispered.

Ex me accuse.

There was no way she was correct. She was obviously having a profound misunderstanding; a cosmic misunderstanding. Still, she was shaking so hard she could barely hold the pencil with which she was now writing Arturo Pesavento's full name on a Post-it note. Why was she doing this, what was she going to do with this precious name once she managed to write it legibly?

Leg ably.

Beg lily.

"Hush!" she said out loud, realizing what she had to do, the only way to still her shaking.

The Pesaventos lived in an old brick row house in a painfully quiet neighborhood bordering the cemetery, the sidewalk out front meticulously swept, the graffiti across the street only mildly offensive. A few slim, troubled trees fought upward from the squares of soil allotted them. The sound of a bouncing ball echoed down the empty block as though it were being dribbled by the last living person on earth, though Josephine didn't see anyone dribbling a ball.

Arturo Pesavento was sitting on the cement stoop of the house. A plump ten-year-old boy with thick black hair in a bowl cut and a chin sticky with recent Popsicle. He held a portable video game.

She was overjoyed. It had been so easy, to find the address

online, to come here, to see him, to reassure herself. She had to stop staring, she knew that, but she couldn't help it.

"What you staring at?" he said, glancing up from his video game.

She was tongue-tied, deluged with relief. She would stand guard here the rest of the day, make sure no truck veered up onto the sidewalk, make sure he went to bed tonight in the same impeccable shape in which she now found him.

"You got a staring problem?" he barked.

"The . . . trees," she said. "I'm doing research on the cherry trees."

"Okay," he said, relaxing a bit, returning to his video game, "but they're crapapple trees."

"Okay," she said. He looked so healthy, so vibrant, punching away at his little machine, a million miles removed from his death.

"Die, dude!" he muttered victoriously at the screen. "I won," he informed Josephine, arching his back to crack it.

"And how old are you?" she said, awkwardly.

He seemed to consider not replying.

"Eleven," he finally said.

"Eleven?" Her throat tightened. "Aren't you ten?"

He wrinkled his forehead and looked at her.

"No," he said, almost patient. "I'm eleven."

"I'm sorry," she said. Perhaps she'd made a mistake with the dates. "I thought you were ten."

"I'm not ten," Arturo Pesavento said darkly. "My *brother* was about to turn ten."

"Your brother," she repeated, as the Pesaventos' home became extra-vivid before her. How had she failed to notice the sagging GET WELL! balloons tied to the window bars, the altar surrounding the miniature blue Virgin cemented into the pavement beside the stoop, the soggy teddy bear and the ribbons and the notes and the soccer trophy? Why hadn't she wondered why a kid his age wasn't in school at this hour on a Monday?

Arturo Pesavento's older brother grabbed his video game and marched up the steps to the front door.

"Go away," he snapped. "Please!"

As she turned away from the Pesaventos', a man in a gray sweatshirt strolling down the sidewalk across the street looked over at her and smiled.

FIFTEEN

The cemetery was strangely hot, Indian summer loitering over the graves. Even the marble angel spewing water into the pond looked dehydrated.

And it was hurtfully beautiful: the soft undulating hills like those in the hinterland, the motionless trees, the orderly lawns. Four hundred and seventy-eight acres of grass and death, half a million bodies beneath her feet, her molecules presumably engaged in some sort of exchange with their molecules. The soles of her feet buzzed.

Names, endless names, names given an instant of attention

before attention slid elsewhere; a familiar enough sensation for her, to be alone with thousands of names. The headstones glittered in the sun. Acanthus Path, Monarda Path, Spirea Path, Laburnum Path, Woodbine Path.

Lub burn em.

Would bind.

By the time she noticed her thirst, she was already dizzy. She forced herself to the top of a hill and sank down woozily in the shade of a family tomb.

She was going to vomit; she prepared herself; she was ashamed; the feeling subsided. She rested her head against the cool stone.

Fool throne.

She lifted her head back up. What was wrong with her, using a gravestone for a pillow? She wanted to apologize to the dead for her irreverence. She wanted to apologize to herself for apologizing to ghosts who could very well follow her home.

Standing up felt like an act of tremendous will. She walked around to the front of the tomb.

BOOMHAVEN

Boom, haven!

Her haven–tomb; another deathly coincidence, just like the ones she had been so keen to find in the Database.

She wished her last name were Boomhaven. A name for someone who could ferociously defend herself and her loved ones. Josephine Boomhaven, superhero, examined the list detailing the contents of the tomb.

MATTHEW JAMES BOOMHAVEN B. OCTOBER 3, 1872. D. AUGUST 17, 1918.

HARRIET ROSE BOOMHAVEN B. JANUARY 11, 1876. D. JUNE 27, 1942.

EDITH ROSE BOOMHAVEN B. MAY 18, 1899. D. MAY 18, 1899.

She reached out to touch MAY 18, 1899 and MAY 18, 1899. The engraved lines chilled her fingertips.

BDBDBD.

DBDBDB.

She refused to think about the child, its brief brush with life, the forty-three bereaved years that must have followed, the number of decades it had been since anyone had taken note of the fugitive existence of EDITH ROSE BOOMHAVEN.

Dearth rose boo have.

Instead, she unzipped her bag and looked inside for something to write on. The only paper she could find was a receipt from the Four-Star Diner. Carefully, she copied down the full names, the "B" dates, the "D" dates.

It wasn't much of a plan, but it was a plan.

Once she had finished writing it all out, she folded the receipt, placed it in her wallet, stood up, strode down the hill. Wintergreen Path, Yew Path, Hill Path, Mahonia Path, Prim Path.

Then, a double headstone: J NEWBURY, twice.

She resisted, but the magnetic letters won, pulling her off Vernal Path.

Upon closer inspection, it proved to be JANE LOUISE NEWBURY and JONATHAN PHILIP NEWBURY. They shared a burial date: NOVEMBER 4, 1870.

A couple together burning in bed, a couple together pocked with plague. The indifferent sun. Sunburn blossomed on her hot cheeks. A headache blotted her vision red. She staggered lost among the graves until she reached the black wrought-iron fence. On the other side of the fence, people strolled and children licked cones. The miraculous ice cream truck. She walked alongside the fence, clinging to its bars, hoping for a gate.

The smells of the world assailed her—grass rotting, dogs peeing—yet even so a monstrous hunger rose within her. She needed ice cream, cottage cheese, chocolate, rice, milk, licorice.

SIXTEEN

She knew he wouldn't be in the cellar when she returned. She knew the rooms would be sunk in shadows, the bathtub haunted, and she would sit in the dark the whole night, starving alone. Her joints ached, or maybe it was her brain. She limped up the block toward the sublet.

He was there. The lamps were on. Something steamed on the stove. She stood in the doorway in disbelief.

He came over to her. He smiled the smile of someone who didn't spend his days typing death dates into a database. He relieved her of her bag.

"You look like you need a hug," he said.

She felt like an alien. As though she had never before been exposed to the way things are done on Earth: that you can return home to someone who cares for you, that a few overused words can hurt your heart with their appropriateness, that your muscles can soften into the muscles of another human being.

"I got you something," he said. She wanted to cry out when he pulled away from her.

He went to the fridge and returned with a Coca-Cola in a bottle. Coca-Cola in a bottle was one of her favorite things. He twisted the cap off with the bottom of his T-shirt and handed it to her. He was good as gold, good as ever. She drank hard, the carbonation burning her throat.

That you could have a need; that someone could bring you something to fulfill this need.

He reminded her of a funny story from their past involving an old friend, someone mistaking vodka for water, connected to a later story in which Joseph disguised Guinness in a Coca-Cola bottle; you had to be there. She was shocked by her laughter. She stroked the cool perfect lines of the Coca-Cola bottle.

Oca ola otto.

"I hate my job," she allowed herself to say, as though she meant it in the way people usually mean it. "You hate yours too, right?" Misery loves company.

"It's boring," he said. "But it's great, in a way."

She was not in the mood for him to elaborate.

Later, they sat on the couch, eating carrots. She leaned her head against his skull while he chewed. She listened to his jaw moving. She liked to hear the sounds of his skeleton.

SEVENTEEN

Alone in the ungenerous light of the elevator on Tuesday morning, Josephine pressed the DOOR OPEN button again and again. The elevator had stopped on the second floor, as per her request, but now refused to release her. Instead, it began to rise at its stately, maddening pace. It stopped inexplicably on the eighth floor, the tenth floor. The doors remained sealed. The elevator then descended, stopping on the seventh floor, where the doors opened into the desolation of an empty hall. On the way down to the basement and on the way back up to the tenth floor, Josephine attempted to exit on floor two.

The even floors, she realized, were all locked. The File Storage floors. The floors with the dusty bathrooms that Trishiffany had maligned within minutes of meeting her. Like the floor she had tried and failed to access in her search for the vending machine.

Tucked into her bra, damp with her anxious sweat, the Four-Star Diner receipt bearing the names and dates of the Boomhavens.

She was operating under the uncertain assumption that the second floor should contain file storage for the earliest letters in the alphabet. But the second floor continued to elude her. She rode the elevator up and down, up and down, up and down. She had arrived before business hours, but now business hours had begun. Occasionally other bureaucrats joined her on her upward journey; all exited on odd floors.

She knew the gray files were mounting in her office, beginning to bury her desk.

A bureaucrat with papery skin and flat eyes boarded the elevator, pressed the 2, and swiped a card across a keypad that Josephine had neglected to notice. The elevator doors, now cordial, opened onto the second floor. The zombie bureaucrat headed down the fluorescent hallway, unaware of her.

A surge of joy, a surge of panic; Josephine rushed out of the elevator. This could have been the ninth floor or any floor—the same concrete, the same metal doors. But these doors, unlike most, bore labels: small typewritten signs taped just above the handles.

She felt so victorious, so shrewd, when she saw that the first door read AA–AE: correct, finally.

AAAE.

AEEI.

EIEIO!

She wanted to jog down the hall, but she made herself walk the bureaucrat's walk, the weighted scurry.

Easier than she could have dreamed: Here it was, the door labeled BL-BR. First she tested the handle—not locked. She braced herself, shoved her body against the door, tumbled into the room when it slid smoothly open.

Blushing, she closed the door behind her and turned to confront File Storage BL-BR. The room was unlit, murky. She'd gone three steps when a light clicked on. She froze; then realized the light was controlled by an automatic sensor. Now a single pale bulb in a wire cage illuminated a tiny fraction of the room. It seemed impossible that such a cavernous space could lie behind a door identical to the one that led into her office. Aisles of metal shelves loaded with boxes of gray files stretched upward toward an unseen ceiling.

Josephine stepped into the first aisle. A second light clicked on, startling her briefly, followed by a third, a fourth, as she passed boxes of files labeled with multi-letter combinations. It was uneasily warm, dense with dust. She walked down the aisle, moving from lightbulb to lightbulb. Vast rows of BLAs, aisles and aisles of them, and then the BOAs (the BMs and BNs a blip), the BOBs, the BOCs. Finally she gave in and ran, lightbulbs snapping on to keep pace.

And here she was. The BOOs. The BOOMs.

Boo.

Boom.

Boomshakalaka.

Once again, exceptional good luck: The BOOMH box was not on one of the impossible shelves, those that receded away into the great dimness. It was on a shelf almost but not quite out of her reach. She stretched toward it. She felt vigorous, powerful, in possession of abundant inner resources. She engaged all the muscles in her arms; she placed the box on the floor.

These gray files were like all the gray files she had known in this place. As she flipped through the box, a file sliced her ring finger, but she paid no mind to the slender line of blood.

Here they were, her three BOOMHAVENS, the only three, right in front of the BOOMHOWERS. She was trembling.

Matthew James Boomhaven. Harriet Rose Boomhaven. Edith Rose Boomhaven.

She pulled the three files, spread them open on the unfinished floor. She reached into her bra for the receipt. The form hadn't changed. There they were, the typewritten dates, the "D" at the top right, the "G" ending the second row, just as she had feared: D08171918, G10031872. D06271942, G01111876. D05181899, G05181899.

She closed her eyes and knelt before the files in understanding, in grief. She felt her fantastic strength draining away.

When she reopened her eyes, she inched toward Edith's file, which she noticed bore only a small fraction of the chaotic text customary for the fifth line of the form: S*(8X&^P=+/–. Edith, never-more-than-newborn; Edith, whose life ceased within twenty-four hours of her birth.

Josephine rested her mournful eyes at the end of Edith's third line, the line that began P/G01221872 and ended D08171918.

That 08171918 itched at her for a sluggish, stupid moment, until she recognized its source. Alert again, she examined the fourth line of Edith's form, which began M/G04151875 and ended D06271942.

It was obvious now. Paternal death date. Maternal death date.

She wanted the first date on the third and fourth lines of Edith's paperwork to be her parents' birth dates; she craved that tidiness. But now she would figure out for certain what those dates meant—she would scrutinize these godforsaken pages forever until she understood everything.

Then, the sound of someone walking, the sharp noise of shoes coming across the massive aisles toward her, caged lightbulbs clicking on accordingly.

She stopped breathing, didn't dare shift the form in her hand lest even that minuscule noise give her away.

EIGHTEEN

"Jojo doll," Trishiffany said, rounding the corner in a fuchsia suit with matching stilettos. Her eyes were more bloodshot than ever. "You so shouldn't be here."

"It's you!" Josephine said, relieved.

"You look terrible, Jojo," she said. "What's wrong, doll? Your eyes! So bloodshot!"

"I realized what I do here," Josephine said, gesturing outward at the complex as a whole.

She hoped Trishiffany would probe into this declaration, would tell her that she was mistaken, that she'd misunderstood everything (silly Jojo!), that she wasn't the bureaucrat queen of death dates.

Instead, Trishiffany nodded.

"Of course you did, doll. You're plenty smart. It was only a matter of time."

"I refuse."

Free use.

Fuse re.

"Yes, we all have that moment. But if you don't do it, Jojo doll, someone else will." Trishiffany leaned against the metal shelf and rested her cheek on a box of BOOs. "You're very good at your job. Very precise, very discreet. You can do it with more compassion than others might. In the town where I grew up, the man who owned the funeral parlor gave a lollipop to every child who passed by."

The lightbulb glared down on both pairs of bloodshot eyes.

"Anyway, sometimes you get to see nice things happen," Trishiffany continued. "Remember Viola Pink Olguin? Alive and well. Thirty-three years old. The chemo worked, the car didn't skid, who knows. But bless her."

"I can't do it." Josephine coughed; the dust.

"You're not *doing* anything, Jojo doll. You're just inputting data. Keeping things up to date. That's all."

"So who picks the dates?" Josephine demanded.

"Things get closed out when the time comes for them to get closed out. The same fifty-seven thousand or so people die in this city each year, the same fifty-five million or so die on the planet each year, Josephine Newbury or no."

Josephine became aware of her own teeth chattering.

"Don't you mainly just want to have a good life with your husband and kid where you don't have to worry about being unemployed?"

"I don't have a kid," Josephine said bitterly.

"There's two days' worth of files drowning your desk right now." Her words were severe but her voice was serene. "I highly recommend that you hightail it to 9997 and deal with that situation."

Trishiffany met Josephine's cold gaze, her eyes warm with sympathy; was that the sheen of tears?

Trishiffany retrieved Edith's sheet from between Josephine's fingertips, restored it to its file, picked up all three BOOMHAVENS, re-filed them, returned the box to the shelf.

Josephine covered her face with her hands.

"Oh, don't do that," Trishiffany said. "The oils on your hands are no good for your skin. By the way, have you ever tried Pure-Pore? It might help you. It can be hard to maintain healthy skin under these circumstances. I've developed a daily skin regimen."

Trishiffany was a wizard with makeup, but when Josephine looked hard, she could tell that her skin too was struggling, the texture of a breakout rough beneath the layers. The sight filled her with pity, for herself and for Trishiffany, stuck in this place without windows, pushing fatal paper while their skin and eyes degenerated, while they degenerated.

"Thanks for the tip," Josephine whispered. "PurePore."

"That's what I'm here for, Jojo doll," Trishiffany said. "Okay, let's rock."

Yets lock.

She pivoted on her stilettos and led Josephine down the aisle in the direction of the door.

Back in 9997, Josephine stood beside her desk, eyeing the accumulated files, dizzy. A bead of sweat rolled from her armpit down her torso. She did not dare touch them. Like snakes. Handle with a stick, avoid skin contact at all costs.

NINETEEN

On Wednesday morning, Josephine did not get out of bed. She did not put on her underwear, her tights, her skirt, her blouse, her sensible shoes, her cardigan. She did not go the bathroom; she did not brush her teeth.

She had prepared her lie (a presumed fever, nausea, the beginnings of the flu). She would never tell him the truth about her job; she didn't want him to be poisoned too.

But he scarcely seemed to notice her lethargy.

"Go on without me," she said from the bed. "I'm not going to work today."

"I see that," he said. He kissed her forehead.

She awaited his solicitous questions, any expression of concern, but he just stood there pulling on his jacket and looking dimly pleased with himself, like a man headed out for a breakfast of croissants and café au lait with a ravishing mistress.

"Rest up," he said with a wave. She couldn't tell whether the words sounded hollow or if her own ear lent them that emptiness.

She closed her eyes, trapping her tears, and gave herself permission to float, to imagine café au lait or wine in a plaza in Spain, bright music, people dancing, someone encouraging her to dance. But all she saw when she shut her eyes was her office, three days' worth of gray files devouring her desk, the bruised pink walls sighing, pressing in toward the humming computer.

By midmorning her physical state had slipped to match her lie; she felt feverish, queasy, permeated by illness. It took her half an hour to convince herself to stand up, go to the bathroom, drink water. There was a spider in the sink.

"Hey," she said to the spider.

The spider looked up at her.

"Hi," the spider said. "Man, you should really go back to bed. You look terrible."

"Thanks," she said, sarcastically or gratefully; even she couldn't tell.

She lay in bed. A scrap of sunlight journeyed down the window well and across the butterfly quilt. The bed spun slowly in a circle, clockwise; then it spun slowly counterclockwise. The ceiling began to undulate.

Undue late.

Ulna duet.

Luau dent.

Dual tune.

Do la nu.

Duel aunt.

Laud tuna nut.

A dune lute.

"Please," Josephine begged. "Silencio!"

Ice in sol!

Lice is no!

Slice eon!

An enormous black dog stood in a shadow in the park, waiting to attack, silent and beautiful. Panicking, she sprinted away and jumped into a car. She began to drive, even though she had forgotten how to drive. She ran a red, got trapped in an intersection, caused a traffic jam, merged onto a superhighway, one of those immense twelve-lane highways of the hinterland. She was going to have an accident but at least she was alone in the car. Then she glanced in the rearview mirror and realized she was driving a bus filled with a hundred billion people.

"You can quit!" she shrieked at the ceiling.

TWENTY

On Thursday, she commuted with Joseph as usual, in her typical tame skirt and cardigan, pretending today was a day like any other. After a morning spent sitting in her chair, ignoring the avalanche of gray files on her desk, not daring to move, barely daring to blink, she finally stood up just after noon, exited the room, and marched down the hall to the office where her interview had taken place.

"Come in." The voice as dry as ever.

Much to Josephine's surprise, the desk was covered with a white tablecloth and set for an elaborate luncheon for two, each of the four courses guarded beneath its individual metal dome.

A carafe of water, a stainless-steel coffeepot, cloth napkins, multiple spoons and forks, a pair of salt and pepper shakers, a pitcher of cream, a basket of rolls.

The smell of the bad breath filled the room, worse than ever; Josephine half-expected to spot a small dead creature on her boss's tongue.

"Pardon me," Josephine murmured, relieved that she had an excuse not to enter. "I didn't mean to interrupt. I can come back later."

"Please sit, Ms. Newbury." There was still that vagueness to the face, the skin chameleoning into the gray walls until the mouth seemed almost to float unmoored in the air. The right hand gestured toward the second place setting, then grasped the carafe and filled both water glasses.

Josephine blushed, hesitating in the doorway.

"The table is set for you, Ms. Newbury," The Person with Bad Breath said with a smile either kind or grim, impossible to decipher. "I have been awaiting you."

Alarmed but obedient, Josephine closed the door behind her and sat down.

"Please, enjoy your soup." The Person with Bad Breath removed the twin metal domes over their soup bowls.

It was a green soup, split pea perhaps; Josephine's fingers were weak on the handle of the spoon. She tried and failed to focus on her sizable hunger rather than on the smell emanating from her companion, now worsened by its partnership with the flat overcooked odor of the soup.

"I would like to take this opportunity to thank you," The Person with Bad Breath said, spreading butter on a roll, "for your service."

Sir vice.

Josephine lifted her second dome, focused on the limp cucumbers and pale tomatoes of the salad, her eyes craving any sight other than those arid lips. She took refuge in draining her water, looking at her lunch companion through the shield of the bottom of the glass.

"Have I ever told you, Ms. Newbury," The Person with Bad Breath continued jovially, "about my pets?"

Spy pest.

As it turned out, The Person with Bad Breath owned two cats, sisters, thirteen years old, but with very different personalities. Wasn't it funny that Lucky was charming while Charm was a misanthrope. Josephine couldn't help but picture the cats as faceless, their little fangs floating.

The cat monologue carried them through the main course— an overly creamy fettuccine Alfredo of which Josephine ate three bites—and delivered them at last to the sticky, sickly cherry pie.

"I could eat this pie forever," The Person with Bad Breath declared, and then, with a wave of the fork toward Josephine's untouched dessert, "Mind if I assist you with that?"

Josephine shook her head no, and her boss devoured her pie.

"I quit," Josephine said.

"Did I ever tell you about Lucky and the pumpkin pie?" The Person with Bad Breath untwisted the top of the saltshaker and took a swallow of salt.

Josephine stared.

In the same casual manner, still rambling about Lucky and Charm, The Person with Bad Breath untwisted the top of the pepper shaker and gulped some down; licked all the pats of butter off their foil wrappers; drank the remainder of the cream straight from the pitcher.

"And that," The Person with Bad Breath concluded, "is why I had to attach an air freshener to Charm's collar. You can't quit."

"This is a free country, isn't it?" Josephine said with a flare of rage.

"True." The Person with Bad Breath picked up the dome with which Josephine had covered her fettuccine Alfredo when she set it aside. "But you are someone who has yet to use herself to her full capacity."

Josephine was paralyzed, unable to respond.

The lips twisted up into a mysterious, parched smile. The fingers twirled a fork deep into the pasta.

"Go ahead. Leave now if you must," The Person with Bad Breath said. "Take Friday off; we will see you back here next week."

TWENTY-ONE

"Let's get going," Joseph said as he came through the door of the cellar after work on Friday. She was sitting slouched at the kitchen table, clinging to a mug of tea, as she had been when he left for work—"I need some extra time to get ready today," she'd lied, "just leave without me, it's fine."

"Going?" she said now with her unused voice.

"You okay?" He looked hard at her.

"I'm fine," she said.

"No," he observed. He came over and stood behind her and

cupped her neck with both hands. "But at least it's the weekend. Work okay today?"

She nodded as though she hadn't spent all day creeping around the apartment.

The stranger to whom the garden apartment belonged would return over the weekend, and Joseph had found a third sublet for them—a place that promised to be better than this one, a little bit more per week now that they were doing a little bit okay financially, one neighborhood over and slightly farther from downtown, but still on their train line. He alleged that they had discussed all this quite recently, though she could retrieve no such memory from her blurred brain.

"Where's the duffel?" he said, heading down the dim hallway toward the bedroom.

The owner of the third sublet had described it to Joseph as being "beside the bridge"; when the taxi dumped them and their stuff on the sidewalk, they discovered that the bridge was really an entrance ramp onto the highway.

A new stranger's door, a new poorly lit hallway, a new set of keys with which to fumble. Inside, they found a room filled with plants, fifty or more plants, ranging from a cactus to a miniature orange tree; plants in pots, plants suspended from the ceiling. The air was damp, sulfuric.

Joseph plopped down on a stained couch lodged among the plants. A hanging fern dangled above his head like a spiky green hat.

"Do I look pretty?" he said.

At other times in their life she would have laughed. He tried to open the window to let in some air, but it jammed after just an inch.

She turned on the hall light, which burned fiercely for a few seconds before popping into darkness. In the dark, they couldn't locate any spare bulbs.

"What did we do to deserve this?" she said.

"We broke someone's heirloom plate," he said.

She looked over at him, but it was too dark to tell whether he was being funny or serious.

Late in the night—after they'd bought lightbulbs at a bodega, after he'd managed to say something that forced her to smile, after they'd found a pizza place ("hint of hinterland," he observed when the pie arrived thick-crusted)—he held her tightly.

She was feeling kinder, despite the poisonous fragrance of the plants; she was about to murmur "041-74-3400" like a term of endearment.

"Don't be a stone," he said. "You can't be a stone anymore."

Tone y tore.

Only ore.

She pulled away from him, confused, offended.

It was a rainy weekend. She appreciated the appropriateness of the weather. They slipped into a kind of mute peace. She kept her mind bland, hardly thought about her office, the gray files piling up toward the ceiling.

On Sunday night, they went for a walk. The rain had given way to a light mist. They were passing a Catholic church and convent with a FOR LEASE sign when it began to pour again. As they grappled with their shared umbrella, she sensed another couple walking annoyingly close behind them, their shadows overlapping with hers and Joseph's. That couple was also struggling to make an umbrella cover two.

In the churchyard, a spotlight glared up at a marble statue of Mary. Above the statue, a single rain-battered tree scattered leaves as fragile as discarded tissues. Beyond the leaves, red stained-glass windows gleamed dully. Josephine imagined nuns with candles, gliding insomniacs, terribly beautiful, terribly silent, pretending the FOR LEASE sign didn't exist.

Glancing behind, she realized that the couple following too near to them was in fact them—an illusion born of the conflicting shadows cast by the streetlights. She looked down at the sidewalk and tried to parse the disorderly shadows, but she got distracted by something: shining slimy in the streetlight, a proliferation of drowned worms, enough worms to make one's gut tremble.

She decided not to mention the worms. She didn't want him to have to know about all the worms they couldn't help but step on, all the remnants in the treads of their shoes.

TWENTY-TWO

On Monday morning, Josephine got dressed for work. She stood in the bathroom with Joseph. There was a row of plants on the rim of the bathtub, bamboo and other things. As they brushed their teeth they made bug-eyed faces at each other in the mirror. She was absorbed enough in the face-making that it was a moment before she noticed the pitiful state of her eyes, her skin. She spat.

She was dressed for work. It seemed that she was going to go to work. It seemed that she was going to sit down at her desk, enter her password into the Database, reach for a file from the hill of files.

But she lingered as he put on his coat.

"You coming?" he said.

"I need a few more minutes," she said. "Go ahead without me."

He hugged her, but breezily, and was gone. She stood, unmoving. She was going to go to work. She ran to the door, about to yell for him—wait for me, I'm ready. But something caught her eye when she opened the door: THIRD DELIVERY ATTEMPT FAILED.

Tempt paled.

Lent ailed.

She yanked the postal notice off the door, ripped it in half, separating the JOSEPHINE from the NEWBURY. No one knew this latest address.

Walking in the park, Josephine tried to imitate a happy person, a satisfied, relaxed, competent person strolling in a park, but she kept having the sensation of people staring at her. A small girl with a soccer ball. A skinny woman whose black pit bull strained against its leash. The frightening old men who dared fish in the city pond. All staring at her, or so it seemed, with brazen judgment, as though they knew she was not where she was supposed to be. As though someone had instructed them to keep an eye on her.

Because the Database had abused her eyes, the swans looked to her like big white irascible blurs. A baby sitting on the grass in a red coat was actually a fire hydrant; a spaniel's face was actually a spaniel's behind.

She feared the pit bull chasing its squeaky toy that shrieked like a human when trapped between canine jaws.

A group of schoolchildren swarmed the paved path; their exhausted teacher pointed them toward the exit. "But we didn't even get the chance to get lost!" a girl protested.

Josephine fled the paved path for a dirt trail leading toward the innards of the park. She passed trees tagged with graffiti.

Discarded soda cans, used condoms, dirty napkins, ragged spiderwebs, squirrels more anxious than usual.

She almost stepped on a matted mash of twigs and feathers twisted at bizarre angles, an appalling object, difficult to look at. Only a sicko would gape, attempt to sort it out, weigh in on one side or the other—a fallen nest or the aftermath of a death?

She came to yellow police tape boxing in the area between three trees, but the space was empty. No blood, no sign of anything.

She hadn't even brought her phone.

She stood eyeing the police tape until a father carrying his young daughter on his shoulders strolled past. "I can't even tell what you're pointing at," he was saying to her, almost scornfully. "Are you pointing at the trees? What, you want us to go and live in these woods and be savages?"

Josephine hurried away from the police tape, emerged out of the woods onto a lawn covered in grazing geese. The geese began to stride in her direction, hissing.

She escaped onto a path lined with cattails.

Scat tit.

At ails.

A row of dead cats all hung up by their tails.

A man and woman in business attire passed in front of her, talking loudly and walking quickly. The man was saying, "and we'll live by a lake. We'll have a boat. A rowboat." The woman looked tired. There was a stain on her cream-colored blouse. "Yeah, yeah, yeah," she kept saying, maybe sarcastically.

And then, on the way out of the park, a mouse in the middle of the road, practically two-dimensional now, its mouth frozen open in a scream.

She wouldn't let the geese win. She would be brave; she would go to the grocery store like a normal person. She would buy food.

She would cook food. She would talk to him. Tell him everything. They would make a plan. As they always had.

She walked and walked and eventually came to a grocery store with a filthy yet friendly yellow awning and a tower of pomegranates out front. She didn't know whether pomegranates should be selected based on firmness or fragrance or hue.

Poor me granite.

Pagan remote.

Page tame no.

She grabbed three at random, and a few vegetables, a box of spaghetti, a chunk of Parmesan. The cashier's collar was crooked, the left side jutting upward. Filled with pity, Josephine averted her eyes.

Back at the sublet by the highway entrance ramp, a number of the plants seemed to be dying. There was a text from her mother: *All okay in big bad city?* The bed was unmade and the laundry ungathered. Enigmatic odors arose from the trash can. In the kitchen, mice had already replaced the piles of turds Joseph wiped away this morning. She found it impossible to be fastidious nowadays. She filled a glass and watered a few of the limpest plants. Had they been given any watering instructions? Had Joseph said something about that when she wasn't listening? She felt guilty.

But she felt bold too, as she sliced the garlic, as she turned on the gas, warmed the kitchen, that soothing smell of boiling pasta. She laid it out, this hard-won dinner, on the battered coffee table. He would be home any second now. She would hand him a beer; he would sink beside her into the stranger's stained couch. They would eat dinner and then go to the movies or some other normal human activity. She couldn't wait. She smiled. She stared at the door.

TWENTY-THREE

Josephine put the pomegranates in a bowl and placed the bowl on the coffee table across from her, as though it were a dinner companion. She sat among the plants and ate spaghetti and spaghetti and spaghetti until she was full. At long last, a little bit full.

She called him and left a voice mail. Afterward she was unsure what exactly she had said; it had been at a high volume, that she knew, and had involved a lot of cursing. For a second she felt fantastic, and then she felt dry, thirsty, and lonely.

She left the sublet, which now reeked of abandonment and dying foliage. The dull dusk had given way to a weird sunset, gray pocked with yellow. Weather for aliens. The temperature had plunged and a fitful wind blew highway dust into her eyes. She thought of the boxes containing her sweaters, her coat. The storage unit—she'd almost forgotten about it. She stood on the stoop of the building, shivered, watched cars travel up the ramp onto the highway. It was hard to believe pomegranates could grow anywhere on this planet.

She walked. She stepped over a small dead creature on the pavement. She stepped into a bar. *At times you have serious doubts about whether you've done the right thing.*

As her third cocktail arrived, she thought guiltily of her Puritan ancestors, walking clear-eyed and clean-livered through fresh fields. She pressed her bag against her liver; a honeybee buzzed inside her. *You have a great deal of unused veracity.* But the wooden bar was so beautiful, glass bottles the colors of precious metals, and now she was shaking hands with joy, hands shaking with joy.

"What I've been worrying about lately—" someone said behind her.

The bar was filling up. Dark rain falling hard in darkness. She wanted to know what someone had been worrying about lately.

"—yes, a house of gold, if you can—"

"—which is the main difference between being—"

"—three! Seriously, *three!*"

Who were all these people?

At the far end of the bar, a man in a gray sweatshirt drank something stiff. When she lifted her glass to salute him, his smile was maybe sinister, maybe benevolent.

Security is one of your major goals in life. Stop now. Drink water. Go home. *But you become dissatisfied when hemmed in.*

"—so she starts to study all this stuff about marital—"

Mary tail.

Martial.

"—caress!"

Care ass.

Carcass.

"—here alone?"

It was a long time before she realized this question was addressed to her.

"No!" The gin added the exclamation point to her response. *You desire the company of others. You have found it unwise to feed yourself to others.*

"So, what do you do for work?" the person persisted. Such an uncouth, painful question. A question like tapping on a bruise, pulling at a scab. The wooden stool melted beneath her.

"Whoa there, lady!"

She wondered where it was, the beloved voice that would transform "Whoa there, lady" into *So some shady.* She drifted toward the door on a glowing balloon of laughter and noise. Deep night had arrived. The sky was no longer yellow. She had to pee. She did a magic trick; she floated down the street elevated several inches above the sidewalk. The sidewalk was damp. There were parts of worms in the bottoms of her shoes. She had to pee. Someone grabbed her arm, jerked her back from the intersection. Tuesday, Friday, Sunday, Wednesday, Monday, Saturday, Thursday. A laundromat, washers and dryers all filled with bright clothing, but the machines static, not spinning. A gorilla in the driver's seat of a parked car. A transparent bird, a snagged plastic bag, a woman's arm vanishing into a brick wall. Three luminous Coca-Cola trucks pulled up to a factory. An aquamarine flicker of tail in the narrow industrial canal; she'd always thought mermaids were limited to salt water. The cruel noise of keys, shoving, twisting, was she at the wrong door in the wrong building on the wrong street in the wrong neighborhood in the wrong city in the wrong state in the wrong country on the wrong planet.

She fell through the doorway onto a couch in a jungle like the lady in the painting. Someone sat in the corner, slowly turning the pages of a book. Everyone knows that only murderers read books in the dark. Thick black hair sprouted from her nipples. She didn't get invited to Trishiffany's wedding. At the DMV they x-rayed her brain and discovered there an insurmountable fear of driving. A blind child crossed the street on a radiant tricycle. There was police tape across the door of her office. *Some of your respirations are unrealistic.* When she asked her parents how long they'd been married, one said *A few months* and the other said *A hundred years.* A demon queen perched atop a skyscraper glared out over a brown city.

Sometime after midnight: wakeful, hot, hungry, bloodshot, regretful, poisoned.

An insect whizzed near her ear. *Bob—bob,* went the insect. *Bob-bob-bob,* increasingly frenetic, enraging her. She flapped at it until it was gone.

Her bag, twisted on the floor beside the couch; her phone, dark in her bag. She pressed the circle and the screen lit to tell her *2:57.*

And to tell her: one voice mail from Joseph.

The insect was back. *Bob-bob-bob-bob-bobobbobbobbobbob!*

"You little insomniac!" she taunted, swatted.

The insect dropped dead, tumbled onto her thigh, its legs bent.

She screamed, then wept. She stood up and went to the bathroom and clung to the sink and threw water at her face.

The voice mail was ninety-three seconds long. For the first eleven seconds, he was talking. His words were muddied beyond recognition. She couldn't even get a sense of his tone—urgent or apologetic or calm or excited or nervous or nonchalant. For the next eighty-two seconds, she could hear him moving around. There was maybe the shuffle of papers or the shuffle of phone being returned to pocket, maybe the hiss of a swan or a woman or a heater, the sound of breathing or the sound of walking, click of stapler or plop of pebble into pond, and then, perhaps, a door being slammed, echoing, oceanic, or perhaps thunder, and then another moment of fuzz before the connection was lost.

She listened to the message three times, harboring hope that the distortion of his words was due to poor reception on her end rather than his, but each time the recording delivered identical indecipherability.

She called him. He didn't answer. She called him. He didn't answer.

I'm not the one who garnished our meal with glass, Joseph said with an indecipherable smile. The air she breathed in her sleep blackened her lungs, yet her dreams contained snow, they contained forests.

TWENTY-FOUR

Josephine awoke pregnant.

It was a lackluster dawn, marks from the couch pressed into her skin like the letters of a strange alphabet. Two of the plants in the jungle were decidedly dead.

She could feel it inside, clinging; almost hurting. She didn't know how she hadn't known until now. The weird hungers, the dizziness. And that irrepressible voice, always twisting her language from within—his wordplay met her unrest, unified now in one being. She placed her hands over her stomach; it was a relief to comfort another living creature. She felt her loneliness lessening retroactively, to know their child had been with her all along.

"Hello," she said aloud, shyly.

Eel ho, the baby replied.

But "baby" was too tame a word for this vitality. Beast, miniature beast, precious perfect beast just emerged from the blackness of the universe, rich with desires.

Her heart beat outrageously, like a tin can being slammed again and again with a rock. The divine, terrifying math.

1

2

4

8

16

32

64

128

256

512

1,024

2,048

4,096

8,192

16,384

32,768

65,536

131,072

262,144

524,288

1,048,576

2,097,152
4,194,304
8,388,608
16,777,216
33,554,432
67,108,864
134,217,728
268,435,456
536,870,912
1,073,741,824
2,147,483,648

There was a twenty-four-hour drugstore down the street. She knew; she didn't need to take a test. Still, at 6:03 a.m. she was perched on the toilet in the stranger's apartment, watching the ghostly blue lines appear.

The joy overmastered the hangover.

"I am so sorry about the drinks last night," she muttered, praying she hadn't ordered a fourth.

Nast light.

Gast fright.

"You!" she cried out, elated.

TWENTY-FIVE

By 6:56 a.m., she was in line behind a mother and three children at the only clinic in the neighborhood with early-morning hours. She gripped her health-insurance card in her hand, newly grateful for her job. She could have waited, researched obstetricians, made an appointment at a proper doctor's office. But instead she'd thrown on sweatpants and torn out of the apartment as soon as she located the clinic in her insurance company's online directory.

Because she wanted to start doing the right thing right away. She had been so negligent. She couldn't wait a day, couldn't wait

eight hours, couldn't wait two hours for someone official to say
it aloud, acknowledge it and make it real. She could only wait
four minutes, and then five, six—beginning to twitch with
impatience—seven, eight, until 7:04 a.m., at which time a nurse
in blue scrubs ambled up to the clinic and unfastened the pad-
lock on the metal grating over the door.

"Doc'll be here soon enough," the nurse said, leading them
into the waiting room.

"My kids got food poisoning or something," the mother said.
"Got chicken nuggets last night and they were all three up all
night throwing up their brains."

The kids giggled.

"Doc'll be here soon." The nurse gestured toward the plastic
chairs lining both sides of the room.

Josephine sat down across from the mother and the children,
who didn't look like they'd been up all night vomiting. They
looked alert, proud to have garnered themselves a trip to somewhere unfamiliar.

On the wall above the children, there was a poster:

BE SURE TO EAT THREE HOURS
BEFORE DONATING BLOOD

What's it like to eat three hours? She was feeling impish. How
do they taste? Like cotton candy or grass or concrete?

The youngest child, a girl, ran across the room and deposited a parenting magazine on Josephine's lap. She spun and ran
away, laughing at herself. Josephine smiled at the girl and then
at the mother, who didn't smile back. But the girl returned a
moment later and climbed into the chair beside Josephine's and
pointed at the sky on the cover of the magazine and said, "Wha
color?"

"You tell me," Josephine said.

"Lellow!" the girl said.

"Blue," one of the brothers corrected, watching from across the room.

Josephine opened the magazine to an ad for all-night diapers. "What color are these?"

"Lellow!" the girl persisted.

"*White*," the other brother said.

"What color is this?" Josephine pointed at a photograph of a heart-shaped cookie.

"Lellow!"

"Red!" the brothers countered.

"What color is *this*?" She pointed at a lemon on a page with a recipe for lemon meringue pie.

"Lellow!" the girl said victoriously.

"That's right!" Josephine said. The girl leaned her head against Josephine's shoulder for one divine instant before darting back to her real mother, who scooped her up and nuzzled her neck. Josephine felt slightly bereft without the small, warm weight of that head, until she remembered about her own child.

Eel ho.

The unmanageable euphoria.

Manamanamanamama.

"Josephine Newbury!" the nurse called.

After the paperwork and the blood pressure and the scale and the pee in the cup, she sat in the cubicle on the crinkly paper, waiting. Unable to wait. Her hysterical heartbeat.

The doctor came through the door, followed by a young nurse in pink scrubs. Josephine clutched the paper beneath her so the women wouldn't see her quivering hands.

"Yep," the doctor said. "You're a little bit pregnant."

Josephine was ecstatic, and then faintly disappointed. She would have given so much for an exclamation point.

"Isn't it either you are or you aren't?" she said.

"Uh-huh. We just check the levels in the urine." The doctor sighed. She looked as though she had already given up on the day. "Okay, so find yourself an OB. Blood pressure looks fine. Stay hydrated."

"Is that all?" Josephine said. "Don't you need to examine me?"

The doctor shook her head. "The body knows what to do."

"Oh, thank you!" she said, immediately forgiving the doctor.

The body knows what to do.

After the nurse followed the doctor out the door, Josephine lingered alone in the fluorescent cubicle. But not alone.

It all unfurled before her. All the doctors' appointments to which she would take this precious beast of hers. All the times they would sit together, the two of them, talking or not, in waiting rooms or on trains or at kitchen tables. All the spaces that would someday hold them as this cubicle held them now.

She was crying.

Cub icicle.

Meld then who.

Eel ho.

Back in the waiting room, the little girl with food poisoning was screeching, trying to twist out of her mother's grip. The mother was screeching too. "I'm helping you! I'm *helping* you!"

The young nurse in pink scrubs sat at the desk. She motioned Josephine over to her with a finger.

"For you," she said with a complicit smile as she handed her a pastel-colored plastic bag.

Josephine seized the bag, the concrete proof, and peered in at a pile of prenatal promotional materials.

"Thank you so much," she said, tearing up with gratitude.

"We get it all for free," the nurse explained.

"Still," Josephine said.

"Congrats, mamacita!" she replied with a wink.

TWENTY-SIX

Josephine stood on the sidewalk outside the clinic, litter and leaves skittering past.

She wanted to start celebrating somehow, now, right away. She had waited so long. She pulled a pamphlet out of the plastic bag: "Your Growing Baby."

At five weeks, your baby is about the size of the tip of a pen. She stared at the illustration: a bulbous blob with no recognizable parts. She tried not to be unnerved.

"Aren't you pretty," she said.

Pre tie.

Eat prey.

She pulled her phone out of her bag and called Joseph, pretending it wouldn't go straight to voice mail. She didn't leave a message. She realized she wasn't lonely. She vowed to do everything she ought to do. She would eat spinach and broccoli and walnuts and pumpkin seeds. She would fatten herself, grow enormous, so that her beast could develop fingernails and teeth, the instruments of savagery. She would provide.

If she hurried home to change, she could make it to work on time.

Back at the jungle sublet, she filled a glass with water and immediately drained it. She would take a shower. She would put on her skirt, her cardigan, her shoes. Yes. She would go to work and do what needed to be done.

In the shower, she soaped her stomach with the greatest tenderness she had ever known.

She was about to leave for AZ/ZA, her hand on the doorknob, when the doorbell rang. She sprang away from the door, then crept up to it again.

It was the mailman.

"Package for Josephine Newbury," he declared.

She accepted it: a medium-sized brown box.

"Signature," he said, handing her a clipboard.

She signed beside the "X."

"Good thing you were home," he said. "Final delivery attempt."

The box could contain a bomb. The return address was a company in England. She stabbed the tape with a knife, peeled away layers of bubble wrap and tissue paper.

A cloak coat the color of mist. Cashmere, lined with cream satin on the inside, an oversize white button at the neck. She pressed the garment to her face: the impossible slickness of the satin, the almost imperceptible smell of a goat raised on faraway green hills. Petite in the shoulders, with a hood generous enough to fit a queen's crown. She had never owned anything this fine.

She picked up the packing slip. A price so absurd it made her snort. The product description caught her eye. *Women's Winter Dawn Princess-Style Hooded Cashmere Maternity Cloak Coat*: the word "Maternity" shocking there amid the other adjectives.

She flipped the packing slip over.

The order had been placed by Joseph D. Jones. Of course. The only person on the planet who had known the address of each sublet.

"Ha!" she said aloud, freed at last from her fear of the postal notice stalker.

She had never known him to be so optimistic. Or so extravagant. Or so risky. To order such a fancy maternity item before she was even pregnant.

But here she was: pregnant.

Walking to the subway, she saw a pot of marigolds atop a parked car. One can always build one's life. The cloak protected her just enough from the chill of the October morning. She stroked "Your Growing Baby" in her bag. Rich with life. *What if you had a moment of absolute happiness right now, right this very second. Come on, give it a try.*

And there it was: a swell of happiness, a flash of happiness.

Happy nest.

Ha penis.

She could live with this, with the gray files piled on her desk;

she could be the one who ferried names from this side to the other. She could—she could see dignity in that. She would steal a name from the Database and give it to the beast. A good, solid, strong, fanciful, flexible name. A name for a beast to do with as it wished—gnaw on, or cast aside.

TWENTY-SEVEN

Josephine twisted the key and prepared to press all her weight against the door of her office. She assumed the accumulated files had reached the doorway by now, blocking passage inward.

But the door opened easily. She was not greeted by the mountain of files that had ruled her imagination. Instead, four tame stacks awaited her on the desk. The calendar was still tacked to the wall as she had left it. The Database hummed as it always hummed. Today the sound struck her as neutral; perhaps even benevolent.

Bene violent.

Bone el vent.

The month had turned, but she didn't flip the calendar. She put her hand on the wall, leaned closer, looked anew for the woman and child in the shadow of the trees.

HS89805242381: This time, her fingertips relished the familiarity of the password.

She picked up the file of EMMITT JUDD ARCHINGTON.

ACHING TORN.

CHANTING OR.

She searched the HS number, cross-checked the information, input the date. Her first file since the emergency batch of airplane fatalities; the first file she had ever knowingly processed.

It was less harrowing than she had anticipated.

She remained calm as the names came rushing up at her. She hardly thought about the fact that each of these files represented someone who had once been born to a mother. She averted her eyes from the line containing the birth dates, protected herself from the ages: the thirty-one-year-old, the seventeen-year-old, the two-year-old. Every name she encountered was a possible name for the beast.

By the time she logged the twentieth file, it was as though she'd never stopped.

She put her hands under her shirt, savored the remarkable warmth.

The silence in her office was so complete she began to believe that everyone had left the building and the city and the world. Only she and her beast remained on this abandoned planet. The bathroom too had become a place of profound and uncanny solitude; she hurried away from there, back to her familiar bruised walls. She started when the heater in the corner released its first hiss of the season.

She was starving before noon. She sat at her desk eating an

oversize deli sandwich, bought to nourish life. Avocado, spinach. As though she hadn't spent all morning doing what she'd been doing. As though she was only the most minor of accomplices.

While she ate, she flipped through "Your Growing Baby," examined the timeline: zygote to blastocyst to embryo to fetus to baby. She looked again at the illustration of week five. She willed the beast to share with her its deep dark coziness. But then she felt ashamed that she, the adult, the mother, was the one seeking comfort; how ridiculous, to ask her own offspring to serve as her shelter.

Even after she finished the sandwich, a vast hunger haunted her.

GRABER/AUDREY/COYNE

GRINNELL/LUCY/SPADE

GUJJAR/HAKEEM/MIR

GURLEY/KAREN/JEAN

HAAGENSEN/DONALD/WINTERS

HABICHT/GERTRUDE/ANNE

HACHEZ/PAULINE/CHIOSSONE

HAGGAS/JAMES/CONNOR

HEAGEL/WILLIAM/ARCHIBALD

HEIERMANN/IRA/ABRAHAM

HIGA/FELIX/CESAR

HOEZEL/JOSEPH/ALEXANDER

HYUN/MIN/SEO

IANACONE/JOAO/PAOLO

IGNOWSKI/ALAN/ALEKSANDER

IKZDA/JENNIFER/SUN

ILIFF/GEORGE/EVAN

IMAIZUMI/KATSUMI/REI

INNIS/GREGORY/BARRON

IRESON/STELLA/JANE

IVASKA/ELMA/ADELE

IWATA/KIYOJI/MASAKI

JABARA/AZARIA/LEYA

JACKSON/MATTHEW/SHANE

JAISHANKAR/AARAL/DAEVI

JAMES/ANIKA/SUMMER

JEANBATISTE/MARCUS/HENRY

JEHLE/LUELLA/WINONA

JEONG/KIMBERLY/SARA

JI/MARVIN/MIN

JIMENEZ/DOLORES/DELGADO

JOACHIM/HEKTOR/BORREGO

JOLIVETTE/ZENA/CRYSTAL

JONCAS/MARION/CLAXTON

JONES/ELIZABETH/CAROL

JONES/JOSEPH/DAVID

JONES/JOSEPH/DAVID.

JOSEPH DAVID JONES.

There are plenty of Joseph Joneses. Plenty of Joseph David Joneses. But the birth date was there. And the death date. Today's date. 10082013.

TWENTY-EIGHT

She sat at her desk in the perfect silence. Her body was doing strange and terrible things—her heart, her bowels, her sweat glands—that made it very difficult to think.

This gray file. Just like billions of others. Its pages cool and quiet. Yet his. His blood and spine, his teeth and hands.

Take it and exit.

She seized the file and ran to the door.

No. Hide it first.

Her fingers were quaking, nearly useless, but she managed to zip the file into her bag. In her brain, the sound of heavy rain.

Don't forget your cloak.

Now go, go, go.

She clutched her bag and ran out into the hallway.

But appear calm!

Against all instinct, she slowed. She exited the building at a sedate pace and strolled down the block, her muscles aching from the restraint.

When she reached the corner, she glanced back at the building. She broke into a run, clinging to the contours of his file inside her bag.

File.

Life.

How had she never noticed?

She called him as she ran. Again and again the automated lady offered the intolerable option of leaving a voice mail.

She ran for a long time, not daring to look behind her. She had stolen something quite precious, the most precious thing on the planet; who knew what they might do to get it back.

Sunbeams reflected brutally off windshields, cars transformed into machines for harassing sensitive eyes, a sudden-onset headache. Her hazy vision interpreted a run-down apartment building as a cathedral. She ran past an old lady in a wheelchair missing one purple shoe. A large man carrying a miniature pumpkin. A naked doll with male genitalia. A line of children in angel wings marching across the street, calling out to one another in Spanish. The whole inexplicable world reminded her of him.

She had no plan.

She had removed his file from the premises—what greater act of courage can be expected of a bureaucrat?

A subway train rumbled beneath the sidewalk, vibrating the lampposts and the blue mailbox and the geraniums on someone's stoop, shattering the illusion that this street was anything more than a humble layer atop tunnels and sewers, rats and rot.

She needed a safe place. Was any place safe?

Only he had been there to witness the dustbin of green shards when she shattered the stranger's heirloom plate.

At least a quiet place. Water, birds.

File!

File!

Life!

Life!

File!

The precious beast sounded agitated, almost frantic.

"It's okay, it's okay, it's okay," Josephine murmured unconvincingly.

A young couple strolling in the opposite direction stared at her.

It had become a soft and mild day, no day for a chase. And there was nothing to back up her suspicion that she was being pursued as she entered the park, no screeching car brakes or heavy breathing behind her.

TWENTY-NINE

She half-expected to find him on the less-than-perfect bench, perhaps holding his phone out to the water, recording the sound of swans. Only when he wasn't there did she acknowledge how much she had been anticipating his presence.

Instead, just the empty bench, its paint in worse shape than when she and he had eaten figs here less than three weeks before.

She sat exactly where she had sat that night. If she could scoot a tiny bit in time, she'd be sitting next to him: unpregnant, innocent, ignorant.

The day was becoming more golden by the minute. Glimmering fall weather that denied death as sunbeams glossed dying leaves. On a log poking out of the radiant water, three turtles stretched their necks up toward the light. She imitated them, the sun a tranquilizing balm on the hidden skin of her throat. But then she tipped her chin back down, frightened by the lulling brilliance of this day, the inappropriate and offensive beauty of the world.

What next?

Life, the beast whimpered. File.

She unzipped her bag and confirmed the presence of his file, though there was nowhere else it could be.

He could die by heart attack.

He could die by car, by bus, by truck, by train.

He could die by gunshot.

He could die by suicide.

She panicked.

"911, what is your emergency?"

"My husband is going to die today."

"Where are you calling from?"

"From the park, but—"

"Which park?"

"The big one, the main park, but—"

"Where in the park?"

"By the lake, but he's—"

"Which lake?"

"The lake with the swans."

"With the swans?"

"Where people always feed the swans."

"What are the cross streets?"

"It's in the middle of the park. But my husband isn't here."

"Didn't you say that you are concerned for his life?"

"But he's not here. I don't know where he is. But I know he's going to die."

"Ma'am," the dispatcher said gently. "Ma'am. Do you need an ambulance?"

"No."

"Do you need the police?"

"I need someone to find my husband."

"When did you last see him?"

"Yesterday morning."

"Yesterday?" The dispatcher paused briefly. "You can file a Missing Persons Report with the Missing Persons Unit. I can give you the number. Do you have a pen and paper?"

Her hand scrambled around in her bag, located a wooden pencil with a broken point. There was no paper except for the form in Joseph's file.

"What makes you believe that your husband's life is in danger?" the dispatcher inquired, possibly out of professional obligation, possibly out of curiosity.

Josephine ended the call.

Aside from the paved path, the distant sound of sirens, the buildings visible over the trees, this could be a lake in the wilderness of the hinterland. Trapped underwater by sticky mud in the shallows, orange leaves more vivid than any other leaves. She looked back at her parents as she ran down the trail at dusk. "Will there be a troll?" she hollered, rounding the rock outcropping, passing out of their sight.

"Josephine!" her mother said, speaking too loudly into the cell phone. The word, the warmth, was enough to unleash a swift quartet of tears. "Josephine?"

"Hi," she managed to say. Where to begin. She touched her stomach, hot with grandchild.

"I have been *thinking* about you! Did you get my text?"

"Yes," she said, not recalling any text. How to ask for help. What kind of help to ask for.

"I'd be so happy if you'd text back to my texts," her mother said.

"Sorry, Mom, it's been—"

"Just a sec, we're repainting the guest room, did we tell you? We were getting tired of that purple sponge print so now I'm re-sponging it yellow. Or really more of a gold. It's classy, you'll love it. Let me put the sponge down, okay . . ."

She could hear her mother moving around her childhood bed-room, then the sound of metal paint can sliding across wooden floor and a soft curse. *"Whoa Nelly!"*

"Just tripped over the dang paint, but no spills," her mother yelled.

"I can hear you, Mom," she said.

"You don't sound good, Josephine. What's wrong?"

"Well, actually—" Josephine felt awash in relief, understand-ing. The woman who loved her most of all.

"Is it Joseph?" The awesome power of a mother's intuition.

"Actually, yes—"

"Oh, I'm sorry to hear it. But there are always ups and downs, you know? Do you have any girlfriends to talk to about it? You've got some girlfriends there by now, don't you?"

"Sure I do," Josephine claimed.

"Okay, so go and talk to those nice girls. That's the best cure for this sort of thing."

A man sat down next to her on the bench, too close for com-fort. He was singing "Proud Mary." She didn't want to look at his face but she saw that his hands were many days unwashed. His right leg bounced frenziedly. Three bright white swans on black water, unless her eyes were wrong. *Big wheel keep on turning, Proud Mary keep on burning.*

"Who's that?" her mother said.

"I should go, Mom."

"Well I should go too, hon. Gotta watch paint dry."

She ran. She ran out of the park. She ran past something. At first she pretended that her eyes were making one of their errors, that it was a fallen ice cream sundae, a smudge of whipped cream, a spreading whorl of chocolate sauce, a drowning cherry. But it was smashed feathers, dark blood, swollen innards, wings extravagantly outflung, slime drying on pavement. She kept glancing back until she felt like a pervert.

Life.

File.

The beast whispered, gasped.

THIRTY

Mercifully, Hillary was on duty at the Four-Star Diner. Josephine spotted her hair through the big window, nothing as orange as that orange; she was leaning across the counter, talking to a customer.

Josephine forced herself to stop running, to enter the restaurant like a normal human being. People were sitting in booths, lingering over coffee and toast, chatting or reading the newspaper or looking at their phones. It was the most tranquil, mundane, indifferent scene in the universe.

No one seemed to notice her urgency as she beelined toward Hillary. And so absorbed was Hillary in studying her customer's splayed palm that she didn't notice Josephine either. The customer was a woman of late middle age, slightly overweight, with a soft concerned face; the type that struggles with constipation.

". . . frequently desire the company of others," Hillary was saying.

Josephine crept closer.

"You have a lot of unused capacity that you haven't turned to your advantage," Hillary said, squinting at the woman's hand. "Disciplined and self-controlled outside, you tend to be worrisome and insecure inside. Sometimes you have real doubts about whether you've made the right decision or done the right thing. You're very critical of yourself."

The woman released a heavy sigh.

"You've found it unwise to be too frank in revealing yourself to others," Hillary continued thoughtfully. "Sometimes you're affable and extroverted, but often you're more wary and reserved. You pride yourself on being an independent thinker."

"Stop it!" Josephine said, reaching between the two of them, breaking Hillary's eye contact with the woman's hand.

"Well hallelujah," Hillary said. "Look who's here!"

"That's *my* fortune!" Josephine said, childish in her despair: She had come here to find out how he was going to die, and now she knew her artificial psychic couldn't reveal a thing.

Hillary wasn't sheepish.

"That's everyone's fortune, sugarplum!" she replied. "Anyway, I'm just a hobbyist."

The customer was looking at Josephine with mild annoyance. "She's a genius," the woman said. "Every word she said, one hundred and ten percent true."

"Even though you have a few personality weaknesses, you're totally able to compensate for them," Hillary informed the woman.

"Here's another Zita for your collection." Luminous with

gratitude, the woman handed Hillary a thin wooden board pulled from her purse.

Hillary examined it, cooing with delight. Then she flipped the board so Josephine could see the painting.

In one hand the witch held a set of oversize keys and in the other an apple. It was one of those awkward folk-arty paintings in primary colors, the proportions all wrong, the head enormous, the mouth off-kilter. The eyes were big and messy, but somehow still looked straight out at you. Either the artist had made a mistake with the lines of the dress or the witch was meant to be a humpback. Josephine hated the painting. The apple looked like a handful of blood.

"Saint Zita," Hillary explained. "The patron saint of waitresses and lost keys."

"Did you know, my husband, he's a plumber, there's a patron saint for him," the woman said. "There's patron saints for frickin' everyone."

"Not for bureaucrats," Josephine muttered.

"Oh sure there is," Hillary said. "You just have to look it up in the index."

"Well I guess I better shove off," the woman said.

Josephine reached into her bag to touch his file. Her panic gave way to an excruciating sadness. Sadness that distorted her senses and transformed all colors into agents of cruelty. She closed her queasy eyes against their aggressions.

Then she was in a booth. Hillary sat close beside her on the red pleather. Was there or was there not a rose fragrance emanating from her royal purple uniform. Once more Josephine had the sensation of people staring at her. They frightened her, the people of the world. She was scared to look up, scared to observe the smiles and frowns on their faces. They were the spies of The Person with Bad Breath. The spoons were too, and the saltshaker, the napkin dispenser, the strand of hair; all of them keeping tabs on her, the thief. Again she shut her eyes.

"Jesus Christ, sugarplum," Hillary said. "It's gonna be okay, it's gonna be okay."

A cold napkin passed over Josephine's eyelids, cheek, chin. When had she ever known such kindness. She dared to open her eyes.

"I have this job," she said.

"Okay," Hillary said, waiting.

"I receive the files of people who are about to die," she continued flatly. "I input their death dates into a database."

She looked at Hillary, awaiting her reaction. Disbelief or horror or mirth?

"The summer I was eighteen," Hillary said, equally flat, "I worked in a photo-development lab. People would drop their film off at the local pharmacy and it would be sent to us to make prints. My main job was to monitor the strips of photos as they rolled out onto the drying drum and then cut them into individual pictures. I saw the craziest things. I saw my best friend's father in a motel room with a woman I didn't recognize. I saw cunnilingus and fellatio, though at the time I couldn't make sense of what I was seeing. I saw dead children in caskets surrounded by their brothers and sisters."

Hillary paused. Josephine craved her voice.

"But the worst was the film the soldiers sent back to their families to get developed in the States."

She paused again.

"That was the worst," she concluded.

Josephine pulled the file out of her bag and set it on the bench between them. It looked innocuous and flimsy, just a plain gray folder; inside her bag it had felt so hot, magnetic.

"This is my husband's file," she whispered. "I stole it."

She opened the file and pointed at the death date.

"You poor thing," Hillary said, staring shamelessly at her.

"What, you think I'm crazy?" Josephine said.

"Look, I'm crazy for my hub," Hillary said. "His last name is Tillary, can you believe it? So when I married him, that was the genesis of Hillary Tillary. Isn't that just the kind of coincidence that makes the world go round?"

"He didn't even come home last night!" Josephine admitted under her breath.

"Oh, that," Hillary said. "I know all about guys not coming home."

Wounded, Josephine looked down at her hand. Her untended nail, her inelegant finger, pressing against his death date.

"You know, I always have great advice to give," Hillary said. "People always come here to get advice from me. I pride myself on that."

Josephine looked up at her, suddenly hopeful.

"But in this case, in this particular situation, I'm sorry, but I don't have any advice at all." She squeezed Josephine's hand. "You'll be fine."

"Excuse me," Josephine mumbled, standing up and trying to push her way past Hillary, but the corner of her cloak was stuck in the seam of the booth, trapping her. A terrible exhaustion, a terrible nausea, overcame her.

She sank back down.

"I think I'm going to throw up," she confessed, longing for the beast to scramble her words, but it kept quiet.

Hillary slipped out of the booth and returned swiftly with a pitcher of ice water and a glass.

"There, there, dear. Drink up. . . ."

Josephine tossed her head back and tried to drink down the queasiness.

". . . someday this, whatever it is, will all seem like it happened to someone—oh, wait a sec, wait a sec! Shoot, I should have known right away! I can always see it in a girl's face! Look, I don't even know your name, but I think you are the cutest little sugarplum mama! I'm right, right?"

"I took the test this morning. And went to the doctor." Josephine was surprised to feel herself glowing. It was wonderful to have someone else know. "And then the postman delivered this maternity cloak!"

"The world sure works in ways, doesn't it?" Hillary said. "If that isn't just the chicest little maternity coat I ever have seen."

"My husband special-ordered it from England," she said proudly, momentarily forgetting that she might never see him again. "It's funny, but he placed the order before the baby was even conceived."

"Well he must have known!" Hillary said with conviction.

"He's just hopeful," she countered, though hopefulness was not a trait she had ever associated with Joseph. "How could he have known?"

"Hey, didn't you just tell me you know *before* people are going to die?" Hillary lifted the pitcher and poured more water into Josephine's glass.

And then there it was, the obvious, miraculous thing: the unreliable cellular connection. The shuffle of papers, the hiss of a heater, the oceanic echo of a door slammed in a corridor. Her small cell of an office balanced on a seesaw with an office at the other end of the endless hallway, the place where the opposite operation must occur. And in that office, a person behind a desk. A very particular person.

A hand stretched over the top of the booth and yanked Josephine's hair hard. Stunned, she gasped and twisted around, knowing it would be The Man in the Gray Sweatshirt or some other minion, capturing her now that she had finally hit upon something essential about AZ/ZA.

But the culprit was a toddler, a splendid kid with a grin as big and round as a Ping-Pong ball. Josephine reversed her grimace. The mother smiled apologetically and scolded her child in a watery language that Josephine didn't recognize.

"You have kid?" the gentle-eyed mother asked.

She didn't know the correct answer to that question. The child reached out familiarly and pulled on her nose.

"Hello there, you," Josephine said.

THIRTY-ONE

S he burst out of the Four-Star Diner into an afternoon so unabashedly golden it was hard to believe anyone anywhere had ever faced a problem. The sun was still high, as though this day were going to last forever and forever.

Running back the way she had come, Josephine discovered that her vision was no longer glazed by the blank stare. Now the world overwhelmed her with its precision: the sheen of a little boy's toy frog, the texture of a woman's violin case, the thickness of a man's felt hat. Her cloak a wing. Dazzled, she ran.

She was six blocks from her destination when she noticed The Man in the Gray Sweatshirt coming down the sidewalk toward her. His sweatshirt as gray as the file in her bag. It was only the two of them, no other pedestrians in sight. A sense of doom arose in her. She tried to run like a woman out for a casual jog, notwithstanding her unsuitable clothing, her flapping bag. Right as they were passing each other, she happened to sneeze.

"Bless you," The Man in the Gray Sweatshirt said, said it like he meant it, like an actual blessing. She wondered if perhaps they were just two very polite passersby. His face bore a look of benevolent indifference: the look of a man in a gray sweatshirt out for a walk on a fine October afternoon. He didn't reach out to grab her, didn't rip her bag off her shoulder.

Still, she couldn't bring herself to say "thank you." Instead, she raced onward, eager to put distance between herself and The Man in the Gray Sweatshirt.

Ahead of her, the concrete compound gleamed poisonous in the late sunlight.

Here it was, the doorway labeled "Z," her first and only point of entry into the compound. She ran past it, farther down the block than she had ever ventured, to the next entrance, with its identical metal door: "Y."

Of course. She felt a lick of hope; now she knew what she was looking for.

X   W   V   U   T   S   R   Q   P   O   N   M
L   K   J   I   H   G   F   E   D   C   B

This had to be the longest block in the city, and maybe the world. She was now closer to Joseph's subway station than to hers.

She stood before "A," looking upward.

THIRTY-TWO

No alarm sounded when Josephine passed through the door labeled "A." The hallway she entered was indistinguishable from every hallway she had ever seen in "Z." She paused, glanced to her right and left: the metal doors, the fluorescence, the sound of cockroaches marching. At the far end of the hall, a bureaucrat scurried from one door to another. The sight spurred her into motion. Stillness was dangerous; a real bureaucrat never pauses. She scurried in the other direction. When she reached an EMERGENCY EXIT door, she pressed through it into the deep silence of the stairwell. As in "Z," the concrete steps led upward with no end in sight. Downward, though, she could see that the steps ended in the basement.

The basement.

If her job took place on an upper floor of "Z," couldn't the reverse job take place in the basement of "A"?

She hurried down the basement hallway, which was like all the other hallways but for its lower ceilings and eerie warmth. It resembled a nightmare but it was not a nightmare; here she was, trying every doorknob, finding each one locked.

Only he had stood on street corners beside her and their piled detritus. Only their two minds in the entire universe contained this same specific set of images: a particular pattern of shadow on the ceiling above a bed, a particular loop of highway ramp circled just as a song about a circle began to play on the radio. Tens of thousands of conversations and jokes. Without him she was just a lonely brain hurtling through space, laughing quietly to itself.

Hush-a-bye baby, she mouthed. To the beast, yes, but more to herself. The beast had been quiet for a while, perhaps resting. It was just as well, though, that the beast didn't hear *when the bough breaks, the cradle will drop.*

She was shocked when the twentieth or so doorknob gave way beneath her fingers. She pushed, and the door swung open.

A baby-faced bureaucrat sat on an ergonomic chair in a bright white office. He eyed her scornfully; she felt again that old anxiety of the DMV.

"I'm from the ninth floor of 'Z,'" she announced. "I've been sent by my superior to check in on an employee who works in this department."

The bureaucrat raised his wilted eyebrows but didn't speak.

"Can you direct me to—" she said.

"Superior who?" the bureaucrat interrupted.

She cursed herself for not knowing the name of The Person with Bad Breath.

"Ninth floor of 'Z,'" she emphasized, attempting to match the bureaucrat's irritability with her own, but even she could hear how juvenile her voice sounded. "It's a rather urgent matter."

"Sorry," the bureaucrat said unapologetically. "I'm not permitted to release any information without clearance."

"Where's your superior?"

"Preparing for a meeting." He motioned with a shoulder toward the inner office, where a colossal bureaucrat could be seen staring at a large computer screen. The screensaver's yellow sphere was morphing into a purple cube.

"May I ask him one quick question?"

"Unfortunately, that's not the way it works." It was hard to believe that this person had a home, a bed, a history; that he existed outside the confines of this office.

"Is there anyone else to whom I can speak?" she said, aiming for disarming formality.

"I'm afraid not."

"Might you please direct me to the office of Mr. Joseph Jones?"

"Around here we identify folks by their HS numbers," the bureaucrat said, though she could have sworn that the briefest recognition passed over his features.

It took her a second to remember.

"I've got his HS number!" she said.

She unzipped her bag, her fingers slippery. The bureaucrat watched as she fumbled to pull the file out.

"You have the file," the bureaucrat observed, mildly impressed.

"HS89805273179," she read.

"Well, considering you have the file . . ." The bureaucrat gave in with a defeated sigh, placing his fingers on the keyboard. "What division?"

"He works in the Department of Birth," she said.

"Oh," the bureaucrat said, removing his fingers, relieved. "I'm afraid I can't help you, then. You're in the wrong department."

Puzzled, she regarded the bureaucrat's face, a face so bored it verged on tragic. Had she misunderstood everything?

Joseph's file was open in her hands. She focused on the second row. G1, G2, G3. The word popped into her head.

"I mean Genesis," she corrected, corking her exclamation mark. "The Department of Genesis."

"What's the HS number again?" the bureaucrat said indifferently, returning his fingers to the keyboard.

"HS89805273179." That number: the number meaning his eyebrow, his toe.

The bureaucrat seemed to relish her agitation as he clicked away on his mouse for several long minutes.

"Sorry," he said, still unapologetic, and for a bizarre millisecond she thought he was informing her that Joseph was already dead. "System's been slow all day."

She kept waiting. Every moment moving Joseph closer to whatever it was that would kill him. Something was happening in her stomach, a tornado of queasiness.

"HS89805273179," the bureaucrat said at last. "He works here."

"Where?" Josephine demanded, triumphant.

"Here," the bureaucrat said.

"I mean, where's his office?"

"I can't release that information without clearance from a superior."

"What?" She was fierce. "We already did this! I have his file, don't I?"

"Rules is rules," he said, offering up a fraction of a shrug.

"Tell me where he is." She slapped the bureaucrat's desk. "It's an emergency."

"*Your poor planning is not my emergency*," the bureaucrat quoted. This time his shrug was even subtler. "Look, I won't call security on you," he added magnanimously.

"Security?" she thundered.

But those seven words had used up all his stores of generosity. "Or maybe . . ." he said, reaching toward the phone on his desk.

THIRTY-THREE

Back out in the hallway, she felt the weight of the entire building above her, as dense and impenetrable as the core of the planet. It pressed down on her, deflating her: just a pair of frightened, bloodshot eyes roving amid the remains of a skin-colored balloon.

Maintain your focus.

Locate 041-74-3400.

"Okay okay okay okay okay okay okay okay," she muttered.

His name a synonym for file.

Correction: his name a synonym for *life*, that's what she'd meant.

Her mind unsteady.

Her gut unsteady, that's what she meant.

Then the footsteps. Not the *tap-tap-tap-tap-tap* of bureaucrat shoes. These were sneaker footsteps. Sneaky footsteps. The footsteps of someone wearing a sweatshirt.

Merciful: a door bearing a picture of a woman in a triangular dress.

The slipping figure on the yellow CAUTION! WET FLOOR sign in the restroom looked like someone preparing for sex or for birth, its androgynous legs flung open with abandon; abandon, the untamable urge, she was kneeling, clinging, heaving herself into a toilet, the tornado whirling her apart, molecules and despair.

The seven minutes she spent trying to pull herself back together passed in hazy, slow-motion desperation. Each minute potentially fatal for him. She cooled her cheek on the toilet seat as she shrank before all the different weapons that could be used against her—the ever-growing headache, the overwhelming pattern of the tile.

"There, there, child," someone said, the voice far huskier than Trishiffany's.

"Trishiffany?" she begged.

Something new had started to happen inside her, waves moving in a different direction. She swirled herself around, diarrhea, swirled herself back down, vomit. She held on to the toilet like it was Joseph, there was something so wrong with her, she was going to die, she could smell the animal stink of it, the shame. But it wasn't her file she'd found, was it, and she remembered about the beast, how beasts make their mothers do all sorts of repulsive things early on, and there was a flicker of joy, and she became less scared, and the cloak embraced her back.

By the time she was done in the stall, the nice stranger had fled. Had there been a nice stranger?

When she emerged again into the relentless hallway, it wasn't easy to walk straight, but the complete emptiness of her gut provided a certain courage, the kind of courage that enabled her not to care about the smell emanating from her mouth as she walked from door to door, jerking madly on every knob, knocking hard like the police when the knob didn't give.

But no one ever came to open any door, and she kept going and going until at long last a doorknob responded to her touch, and she entered a small office with sickly pinkish walls, and said the name of the dark-haired man sitting at the desk beside a stack of gray files.

THIRTY-FOUR

H is back was to the door, his desk flush with the opposite wall. He turned slowly to face her.

Joseph: the one who spoke her best language.

But it wasn't Joseph.

The eyes were a different color, the chin a different shape, the demeanor more delicate.

"Oh," she said, "sorry."

The bureaucrat nodded, his face neutral. His fingers lingered on the keyboard of his typewriter even as he looked at her. She pretended, briefly, that he was Joseph; that this was the one who mattered, the one whose file she was brave enough to steal.

"I'm looking for Joseph Jones," she whispered. It was so hushed in there; even her breathing was an intrusion.

The bureaucrat gazed and waited.

She pulled the file out of her bag.

"HS89805273179," she clarified.

The bureaucrat nodded a second time, his eyes on the file. After an apologetic glance at his typewriter, he stood up. He took the three steps across the office toward her, opened the door, and gestured for her to pass through first.

He led her down the hall, farther away from the restroom. He was not old—perhaps even younger than she—but already his shoulders were capitulating to gravity. He stopped in front of a door and knocked politely, perhaps inaudibly.

They were awaiting a response when she heard the footsteps again, the sneakers. This time they were coming faster, rushing up the hallway. It struck her that she might have led The Man in the Gray Sweatshirt right to Joseph. The sense of doom expanded, exploded through her capillaries. The door handle twisted from the inside.

She turned back to look at her pursuer as she darted into the office. But the hall was empty aside from Joseph's doppelgänger, already hastening back to his own life.

The smallest office in the deepest basement. A quiet, apocalyptic place. It felt forgotten, as though the end of the world had already come and gone.

Joseph stood before her, shocked.

"You?" he said.

"You!" she said.

For the first time, she noticed that his eyes were bloodshot too. Less so than hers, far less than Trishiffany's, but bloodshot none-theless. It was unsettling to think she had been blind to such a detail. She examined his forehead, searching for signs of disruption to the skin, but his face was unmarked. Apparently Department "A" was better for one's skin than Department "Z."

"It's god to see you," he said. "But how in hell did you find me?"

"What?" she said.

"It's good to see you, but how in hell did you find me?"

"You said, 'It's god to see you,'" she said.

"Why would I have said that?"

He laughed. She couldn't control the jubilation that shot through her. For a few seconds she pretended he wasn't going to die today. He looked vibrant, striking, tilting toward demon, his dark hair in a sharp peak on his forehead, his smile wry, vital, the monster who would howl at her deathbed.

"The cloak," he said, reaching out to touch it.

"Don't kiss me," she said. "My breath reeks."

In an alternate universe, she would have required toothpaste, nudity, a bed, a moon in a white sky, seven glass bottles lined up on a windowsill; fortified by all that, it would be easier to tell him what she had to tell him.

But instead here they were in yet another windowless office.

At least he was holding her.

"I'm pregnant," she said to the stubble on his cheek just as he said, "You're pregnant," to her hair.

The beast remained silent, though, dozing even at this critical moment; she would have liked to hear what it would do with the word "pregnant."

"So you already know." Pleased, he pulled back to observe her face. "Are you happy?"

"You processed the file?" she said.

He raised his eyebrows, astonished by her level of understanding.

"I *created* the file," he said, lowering his voice. "That's what I was doing those nights away from you. It wasn't easy to locate all the right information."

A brave bureaucrat traversing darkened hallways, sneaking into classified rooms, while just a couple of neighborhoods away a mistrustful bureaucrat sat panicking on a stranger's bed, walked panicking through a stranger's home, filled up with ungenerous speculation.

"I'm sorry," she said, almost too softly for him to hear.

"There were some hiccups," he continued. "The file got booted back to me late yesterday. That's why I had to stay here last night, to figure out what was going on. The form was missing one critical date. But I put the corrected paperwork in Outgoing early this morning. Our blastocyst will become an embryo any second now."

Under other circumstances, she would have said something loving to him just then, would have found a way to celebrate, turned her fingers into fireworks: his disappearances magnificently explained, their child's precious cells dividing and dividing and dividing inside her. But the other thing loomed, pressing down.

"I work here," she began.

"You?" He was incredulous.

"In 'Z.' "

"In 'Z,' " he repeated, somber. "They swore you to secrecy too, right?"

"In 'Z,' " she echoed, trapped in the three letters, unable to forge ahead.

He cupped her neck with both hands, the way he sometimes did.

How many minutes remained in their life together?

She said his name slowly, as though The Man in the Gray

Sweatshirt wasn't waiting on the other side of the door. She pulled his file out of her bag.

His gaze sharpened as he recognized it.

"I stole this," she said.

"Why would you do that?" he demanded.

She couldn't say it. She opened the file. Her finger, the same finger with which she had stroked him in all sorts of places, the same finger with which she had pointed to hundreds of thousands of other things. But now, here on this page, pointing, complicit with D10082013.

THIRTY-FIVE

The Man in the Gray Sweatshirt was not beside the door when they exited the office. They ran down the interminable hallway that continued from the basement of "A" to the basement of "Z." She reached for Joseph's hand. He did not reach back. There was a force field of solitude around him. He ran a foot ahead of her, sometimes seeming like a stranger, sometimes like her twin. He refused to look at her. She wanted to know what it was that he didn't want her to see: panic, selfishness, loneliness. Humble nervous pitiful human hope. She was thirstier than ever. The beast was mute.

May the beast feel only a warm dark slosh. The file flapped, slapped her wrist. She tried to say something but her lips were quivering, unreliable. The straight unbroken line of empty hallway. Gravity sucked on their soles, pulled on their lungs. Behind them, someone pointed an invisible gun at Joseph's back.

B
C
D
E
F
G
H
I
J
K
L
M
N
O
P
Q
R
S
T
U
V
W
X
Y
Z

Through the EMERGENCY EXIT door, up the infinite stairwell, he always two steps ahead, never looking back.

And now: an EMERGENCY EXIT door opening from the stairwell onto the tenth and top floor of "Z." Don't make a peep. Stop breathing so hard. The hum of fluorescence. Monotonous doors sealed against intrusion.

But what's this. Hold my hand, finally. A door dead center in the hallway, propped open with a wooden wedge, eerily inviting. And here: The words we were seeking. Minuscule font beneath old tape.

THIRTY-SIX

"**W**elcome to Processing Errors," Trishiffany said with a wink. "We've been waiting for ages. We thought you'd never get here, Jojo dolls!"

She sat behind the metal desk, her suit halfway between red and pink. Beside her, The Person with Bad Breath serenely tapped a pencil on the lone gray file on the desk.

The office was similar to Joseph's, to Josephine's: small and windowless. But behind the desk, there were two doors. And this office, unlike theirs, felt eminently placid. These walls, Josephine observed, free of smudges and fingerprints.

"Perfect," The Person with Bad Breath said. "She has his file."

"Just as we expected," Trishiffany said.

"Lock the door!" Josephine commanded Joseph, who stood a step behind her.

"No need," The Person with Bad Breath said as Joseph turned to twist the lock.

"Paranoid much, Jojo doll?" Trishiffany smiled.

"We were followed all the way here by your assassin," Josephine said.

Trishiffany giggled. "Our assassin?"

"The Man in the Gray Sweatshirt. He's been following me for weeks."

"I have a gray sweatshirt," Joseph said.

"Every man is the man in the gray sweatshirt," The Person with Bad Breath intoned.

The words emerged from a gust of breath so noxious that Josephine worried about the beast's well-being; surely there was something harmful in such an exhalation.

"I'm not feeling great," Joseph said, eyeing the file on the desk.

"Take a seat." The Person with Bad Breath indicated a pair of plastic chairs.

"He's dying!" Josephine cried out.

"Not exactly," Trishiffany said.

"What is that?" Joseph said, pointing at the file on the desk but unable to look.

"It's what you think it is," Trishiffany said tenderly.

"What is it?" Josephine demanded, but the cool, dreadful certainty was already propelling her.

She seized the file a millisecond before Trishiffany's manicured hand could prevent her. She backed up toward Joseph, looking ferociously at the bureaucrats, ready to hiss if either of them interfered. But Trishiffany and The Person with Bad Breath remained tranquil as she opened the file.

It contained a single sheet of paper. She was having a hard time looking at it, yet she couldn't stop.

Something caught her eye in the fourth row. Following the M/G, the familiar HS89805242381.

"My password for the Database?" she said.

"Yes, but, more significantly, your HS number," The Person with Bad Breath said.

"You were the 89,805,242,381st Homo sapiens ever conceived," Trishiffany said. "And your child was the 129,285,656,702nd."

"Do you know how many hours I spent sneaking around here in the middle of the night to find your number," Joseph muttered to Josephine.

"One among many transgressions," Trishiffany said.

"Trespassing in a superior's office," The Person with Bad Breath elaborated. "Opening a confidential filing cabinet. Stealing an unauthorized form. Trespassing in File Storage N. Trespassing in File Storage J. Copying down confidential information. Using a superior's typewriter to fill in a form with fraudulent information. Typing fraudulent information into the Database. Persisting in doctoring a fraudulent file and placing said file in Outgoing even after deactivation was requested by a superior. Unauthorized presence on site after hours and before hours."

"On three separate occasions," Trishiffany added.

"What do you expect," Joseph said, "once someone realizes he can create a life?"

"Zygote, Blastocyst, Embryo, Fetus!" Josephine comprehended as she scrutinized the second row.

"Today's our embryo day," Joseph said. He put his finger on the 10082013 following the G3(E).

10082013.

10082013.

"But that's what's no good," Trishiffany said. "See how the number sags below the embryo-date line into the paternal-death-date line? The typewritten text must remain entirely within its appointed space."

Joseph snatched the file away from Josephine and examined the form.

"You did a fine job," The Person with Bad Breath congratulated. "Your work certainly reveals an above-average understanding of the mechanisms. But even the finest counterfeit never made it all the way through."

"She conceived, didn't she?" Joseph protested.

"You're diligent, Joey-Jo," Trishiffany admitted, giving him a sad little smile. "Those must have been some long nights. But things are what they are."

"You typed in your own death date," Josephine whispered in disbelief, pulling the file away from him.

"I was typing in the blastocyst-to-embryo transfer date," he countered. "I was fixing the error that got the file sent back to me yesterday. The first time around I didn't realize I had to include that date."

"Oh, no, Joey-Jo. The file got sent back to you because the system had already identified the falsification," Trishiffany said. "You should have deactivated the file, as per your instructions. Sweetly into the ether, so to speak."

"Instead, you triggered your own death processing," The Person with Bad Breath said.

"Typewriters are tricky," Trishiffany soothed. "Though they do have certain advantages in a system like ours."

"Typewriters are tricky and now he's going to die?" Josephine raged.

"Well, at this particular instant, both facts seem to be true," The Person with Bad Breath said. "Your blastocyst is becoming an embryo on 10082013, and Joseph David Jones is dying on 10082013."

Josephine grabbed Joseph's right hand, clamping his finger bones in her grip.

"But not for long," Trishiffany said lightly. "We'll get everything corrected straightaway. Make it all line up."

"A bit of extra paperwork," The Person with Bad Breath said.

"An annoyance, to be sure," Trishiffany continued. "A touch of heartache. But all shall be well and all shall be well and all shall be well. Why don't you hand over those files, Jojo doll."

Josephine shook her head. The fluorescence illuminated every flaw in each bureaucrat's skin. She could feel it gleaming over the constellation of zits on her forehead. The whole world smelled like The Person with Bad Breath.

"It's just paperwork now," Trishiffany said. "Just a matter of sending one file through Processing Errors and deactivating the other."

Josephine's throat released a knotted snarl. Trishiffany didn't acknowledge the sound, the primal disagreement; she briskly clapped her hands.

"Come now, Jojo doll!"

"Why are you doing this to us?" Josephine tried to yell, but the words came out limp, her voice feeble.

Trishiffany released a short sharp laugh. "Nothing malevolent here, dear! We're all just doing what we have to do."

Josephine clung to the files. Joseph rested his head against her head and together they looked down at the blank boxes of their child's form. And then at Joseph's form, the chaos following the first four lines, the boxes of letters and numbers and symbols, the dense forest of his paperwork.

"Let's get it over with, kiddos." Trishiffany's words were flippant but her tone was forlorn.

That forlornness in her voice caused Josephine to loosen her grip on the files. She stepped forward and placed them on the desk.

"Atta girl," Trishiffany said wearily.

"You should sit down, Ms. Newbury," The Person with Bad Breath said, as Trishiffany produced a bottle of Wite-Out from her bra and passed it to her coworker.

The Person with Bad Breath unscrewed the Wite-Out, opened both files, and painted the liquid over the death date on Joseph's form.

"Thank you," Joseph said.

The Person with Bad Breath glanced up, surprised.

"Oh, don't thank me," The Person with Bad Breath said with a dusty chuckle. "There's nothing benevolent here either. I'm not doing favors, I'm doing paperwork. Getting all the ducks in a row."

Then The Person with Bad Breath held the tiny brush suspended above the child's form. Trishiffany breathed in, breathed out, licked lipstick off her teeth. The smell of the Wite-Out merged with the smell of the breath. Joseph looked at Josephine, his face burning with hope, and lunged forward to seize the arm of The Person with Bad Breath.

But the wrist eluded him, the hand fell, the Wite-Out smeared the second row.

The beast had been silent for so long.

"Please sit, Jojo doll."

Josephine sank into the chair, confronting Trishiffany's bloodshot eyes with her own. Aside from those godforsaken eyes and that disguised rough skin, Trishiffany was perfectly beautiful. Put her in a purple robe with a hood and she could stand merciful in a churchyard. She came around from behind the desk. Awkwardly, she ran a finger down Josephine's cheek. Her hand smelled like coconuts and cheap gold jewelry.

"My goodness," she marveled, more to herself than to anyone else, "I could swear your skin's already improving. And look at those eyes."

Deep inside, a fist clenched and unclenched, clenched and unclenched, clenched and unclenched, the weird beat of it interfering with Josephine's breath. With each clench she released a fragile moan; Trishiffany tensed every time.

Marriage.

Miscarriage.

Miss Carriage.

But she was only pretending. It was just her own voice in her own head.

When she opened her eyes, her lap was filling with blood.

The sound grew deep inside her, from the place where she was losing blood, and pressed against all her orifices, shoving itself past her tongue, between her teeth.

"Steady there, Jojo doll," Trishiffany murmured. "You've got to stop that shrieking."

She tried to stop, and eventually she did.

As soon as Josephine was quiet, Trishiffany took hold of her elbow and motioned for Joseph to do the same on the opposite side.

Together they limped toward one of the doors behind the desk. The Person with Bad Breath stood up as they passed and frowned at the trail of red on the immaculate gray floor.

"We'll take care of the paperwork." Trishiffany sounded subdued, fatigued, though her hair was as bright and voluminous as ever. She pressed the door open into a bathroom. "You should have everything you need in there."

"You're both fired, of course." The Person with Bad Breath lifted two fingers to those dry lips and smiled at Josephine, the gentlest of gestures, something somewhere between the sign for "hush" and the motion that precedes blowing a kiss.

"Go ahead," Trishiffany commanded, stately on her stilettos as Joseph guided Josephine through the doorway. "Onward and upward, Jojo dolls."

THIRTY-SEVEN

She sat on the toilet, staring down at the thing that shouldn't be stared at.

He pried her underwear off from around her ankles and put them in the trash can.

Someone knocked on the door.

When he tried to reach behind her to flush, she snarled.

"Okay, okay, okay," he said, lifting his hands above his head like a man held up at gunpoint.

What a companion the beast had been.

Someone knocked on the door.

It had to be her. She had to be the one who flushed the toilet.

"Tell me something," she said.

"The songs we love are dictated by mathematical formulas," he said fearfully. "I didn't tell you when we stepped on worms."

The difficult minutes.

Someone knocked on the door.

But when she threw it open, no one was standing outside.

THIRTY-EIGHT

The Office of Processing Errors was empty. There were no files on the desk.

They walked toward the door propped open by the wooden wedge. She felt something wet on the inside of her cloak. In a trash can somewhere, a positive pregnancy stick still damp with urine. Unsteady, she stumbled over the wedge as they passed through. It slid out of place and the door clicked shut behind them.

But they were not back in the fluorescent hallway as they should have been. Instead, they were in an unfamiliar, ill-lit space.

A caged lightbulb sticking out of the wall directly above their heads illuminated a few square feet, gray paint peeling. The room stretched upward into darkness, vanished into darkness on all sides.

He spun around to open the door. It was locked. He wrenched the handle and cursed.

"No use," she said sedately. Her brain felt soft, her vision blurred, her insides liquid. She was dreamy, devastated.

Beneath the small globe of light they hung on to each other. One of them cried and one of them didn't.

Eventually they let go, turned to face the darkness.

"Wait," he said, pointing forward. "Is that an exit sign?"

She squinted.

"See that red light?"

A distant smudge of red. She didn't trust her eyes.

"I need glasses," she said.

She did feel something though: an almost imperceptible chill wind, grazing her overheated face, stirring the husk of the cloak. She listened to the utter silence inside herself.

He grabbed her hand and pulled her a few steps into the room. The lightbulb behind them clicked off. A flash of darkness. Warmth between their palms. The next bulb clicked on. It was mounted on a metal shelving unit burdened by boxes filled with files.

Her bureaucrat's eye was quick to notice that the labels on these files, unlike all the others she had ever encountered, did not bear a surname followed by a given name. Instead, there were word pairings she didn't recognize: ALLOLOBOPHORA CHLOROTICA, and AMYNTHAS DIFFRINGENS, and APORRECTODEA TUBERCULATA.

She let go of him, floated toward a box of files, lifted her hand to run her fingertips across the familiar gray edges.

"No," he said, pulling her away.

There was a sharp noise behind them, back beyond the door

through which they had passed, a fast pattern of footsteps, stilettos on concrete, talons on metal, and then a massive mechanical click.

All the caged bulbs turned on at once, shocking her brain with light. She had to shut her eyes. A cell twitched, split. A handful of birds or bats swooshed upward in the darkness behind her lids. Something disappeared into the underbrush. Forests' worth of paper. The smell of trillions of sheets of paper, the smell of worms digesting paper, excreting paper.

She dared to open her eyes. The space vaster than her imagination. The metal shelves endless in the light, their relentless geometry expanding upward and outward, vanishing into radiance. Files, forever. Lives and deaths rustling and shuffling and fluttering alongside hers. The outrageous heat of her blood. His hand. Any minute now they would step forward in the brilliance toward the exit sign, past the file of the worm. The file of the dog. The file of the rat. The file of the swan. The file of the turtle. The file of the cockroach. The file of our child, our child. And your file, too.

ACKNOWLEDGMENTS

Thank you, Faye Bender, my agent and my friend, for your vision.

Thank you, Sarah Bowlin, for your editorial genius, which enabled this book to become itself, and thank you to the rest of the Henry Holt team, especially Leslie Brandon, Lucy Kim, Ebony La Delle, Jason Liebman, Courtney Reed, and Maggie Richards.

Thank you to the Rona Jaffe Foundation, which supported this project in its earliest iteration, and to the Ucross Foundation.

Thank you to those who have nurtured my work along the way,

especially Lou Asekoff, Michael Cunningham, Lisa Graziano, Joshua Henkin, Krista Marino, Jenny Offill, Ellen Tremper, and Mac Wellman.

Thank you to the Brooklyn College MFA Program, and to the brilliant members of my writer's group.

Thank you to my colleagues in the Brooklyn College Department of English, and thank you to my students, for your unanswerable questions.

Thank you, David Finston, for the consultation about mathematical matters.

Thank you for your friendship and for your advice, literary and otherwise: Marie-Helene Bertino, Avni Bhatia, Sarah Brown, Adam and Aysu Farbiarz, David Gorin, Camille Guthrie, Lucas Hanft, Elizabeth Logan Harris, Amelia Kahaney, Jonas Oransky, Laura Perciasepe, Genevieve Randa, Kendyl Salcito, Maisie Tivnan, Andy Vernon-Jones, and Tess Wheelwright.

Thank you to my family: my parents Paul Phillips and Susan Zimmermann; my grandparents Paul Phillips Sr. and Mary Jane Zimmerman; my in-laws Gail and Doug Thompson; my siblings-in-law Peter Light, Raven Phillips, and Nate Thompson; my brother Mark Phillips; my sister Katherine Phillips (your presence is felt); and my sister Alice Light, best friend/best reader.

Thank you, Neal, my magical Thanksgiving baby; your company both in utero and out was a good luck charm during the revision of the book.

Thank you, Ruth, my joy, for proudly telling your babysitters "Mommy working on book!" on those mornings when I hardly believed it myself.

And you, Adam: there are no words. Just this book.

PUSHKIN PRESS

Pushkin Press was founded in 1997, and publishes novels, essays, memoirs, children's books—everything from timeless classics to the urgent and contemporary.

Our books represent exciting, high-quality writing from around the world: we publish some of the twentieth century's most widely acclaimed, brilliant authors such as Stefan Zweig, Marcel Aymé, Teffi, Antal Szerb, Gaito Gazdanov and Yasushi Inoue, as well as compelling and award-winning contemporary writers, including Andrés Neuman, Edith Pearlman, Eka Kurniawan and Ayelet Gundar-Goshen.

Pushkin Press publishes the world's best stories, to be read and read again. Here are just some of the titles from our long and varied list. To discover more, visit www.pushkinpress.com.

══

THE SPECTRE OF ALEXANDER WOLF
GAITO GAZDANOV

'A mesmerising work of literature' Antony Beevor

SUMMER BEFORE THE DARK
VOLKER WEIDERMANN

'For such a slim book to convey with such poignancy the extinction of a generation of "Great Europeans" is a triumph' *Sunday Telegraph*

MESSAGES FROM A LOST WORLD
STEFAN ZWEIG

'At a time of monetary crisis and political disorder... Zweig's celebration of the brotherhood of peoples reminds us that there is another way' *The Nation*

BINOCULAR VISION
EDITH PEARLMAN

'A genius of the short story' Mark Lawson, *Guardian*

IN THE BEGINNING WAS THE SEA
TOMÁS GONZÁLEZ

'Smoothly intriguing narrative, with its touches of sinister, Patricia Highsmith-like menace' *Irish Times*

BEWARE OF PITY
STEFAN ZWEIG

'Zweig's fictional masterpiece' *Guardian*

THE ENCOUNTER
PETRU POPESCU

'A book that suggests new ways of looking at the world and our place within it' *Sunday Telegraph*

WAKE UP, SIR!
JONATHAN AMES

'The novel is extremely funny but it is also sad and poignant, and almost incredibly clever' *Guardian*

THE WORLD OF YESTERDAY
STEFAN ZWEIG

'*The World of Yesterday* is one of the greatest memoirs of the twentieth century, as perfect in its evocation of the world Zweig loved, as it is in its portrayal of how that world was destroyed' David Hare

WAKING LIONS
AYELET GUNDAR-GOSHEN

'A literary thriller that is used as a vehicle to explore big moral issues. I loved everything about it' *Daily Mail*

BONITA AVENUE
PETER BUWALDA

'One wild ride: a swirling helix of a family saga... a new writer as toe-curling as early Roth, as roomy as Franzen and as caustic as Houellebecq' *Sunday Telegraph*

JOURNEY BY MOONLIGHT
ANTAL SZERB

'Just divine... makes you imagine the author has had private access to your own soul' Nicholas Lezard, *Guardian*